Donated by
Floyd Dickman

Fresh Off the Boat

MELISSA DE LA CRUZ

Fresh Off the Boat

HarperCollinsPublishers

www.harperchildrens.com

Library of Congress Cataloging-in-Publication Data

De la Cruz, Melissa.

Fresh off the boat / by Melissa de la Cruz.— 1st ed.

p.   cm.

Summary: When her family emigrates from the Philippines to
San Francisco, California, fourteen-year-old Vicenza Arambullo
struggles to fit in at her exclusive, all-girl private school.

ISBN 0-06-054540-2 — ISBN 0-06-054541-0 (lib. bdg.)

1. Filipino Americans—Juvenile fiction. [1. Filipino
Americans—Fiction. 2. Immigrants—Fiction. 3. Moving,
Household—Fiction. 4. High schools—Fiction. 5. Schools—
Fiction.] I. Title.

PZ7.D36967Fr 2005   2004015513

[Fic]—dc22   CIP

                                                              AC

Typography by Karin Paprocki

1 2 3 4 5 6 7 8 9 10

❖

First Edition

This book is dedicated to the amazing DLCs. My parents, Bert and Ching de la Cruz, the funniest and bravest people I know, who inspire me every day; and my siblings and best friends, Christina Green and Francis de la Cruz. With love from the "weird" sister.

And to my wonderful husband, Michael Johnston, without whose love and support this book would not exist.

Acknowledgments

I AM DEEPLY INDEBTED to my awesome editor, Abby McAden, who steered this book in the right direction and took me out to many delicious meals. Thanks to Lexa Hillyer, Martha Schwartz, and everyone at HarperCollins. Thanks to Jennifer Unter for seeing the potential.

I am grateful to Jennifer Kim, Treena Rivera, Karen Robinovitz, and Caroline Suh for their enduring friendship. Thanks to Tyler Rollins, Tristan Ashby, and Gabriel de Guzman for support and encouragement. Thanks to Gabriel Sandoval, Liz Craft, and Justin Manask for making the L.A. transition an easy one. Thanks also to my high school English teachers at the Convent of the Sacred Heart: Dr. Eileen Moriarty, Mr. Joel Ohren, and Mr. Charles Brady, who encouraged me from the beginning.

Many kisses and hugs to the Johnstons—Mom, Dad, John, Anji, Alexander, Tim, Rob, Jenn, and Valerie; the Torre family; the Gaisano family; the Izumi family; the Green family, especially Steve and Nico; and all the very many Ongs and de la Cruzes in the world. And to the memory of my grandparents, *Lola* Eleng, *Lolo* William, Grandpa and Grandma.

While the astronauts, heroes forever, spent mere hours on the moon, I have remained in this new world for thirty years. I know that my achievement is quite ordinary. . . . Still, there are times I am bewildered by each mile I have traveled, each meal I have eaten, each person I have known, each room in which I have slept. As ordinary as it all appears, there are times when it is beyond my imagination.

—Jhumpa Lahiri, "The Third and Final Continent"

"America. Land of the free. Home of the Whopper."

—Balki Bartokomous, *Perfect Strangers*

The Ultimate Loser Move in the Known Universe

THERE HAS GOT to be some way I can just stay in my room until I'm eighteen and have to leave for college. Maybe I can convince my parents to homeschool me so I'll get into Harvard and get written up in *People* magazine. Right. Not going to happen.

Life was fine (okay—not fine, but at least not *terrible*) until last Friday night when I got this brilliant idea to convince my parents to take us to the movies. Movies are a big deal with me, especially since we never go anymore. Mom says we don't have the money and who would pay ten dollars to see a film when we already get three hundred channels on cable? But I begged and begged and begged because I really wanted to see the latest chunky-girl-empowering Drew Barrymore movie.

Somehow, it totally slipped my mind that it was Friday night. This is relatively easy to explain because Friday night is no different from every other night at my house. So it wasn't until we got to the theater that I realized I'd made a huge mistake. The line to get tickets snaked down the hill, and everyone there was my age, hanging out in big groups of friends or on dates, playing with their Game Boys, taking each other's picture with their camera-cell phone, running around or sticking their tongues down the backs of their boyfriends' throats.

While I, on the other hand, was committing the ultimate loser move in the known universe.

I'm fourteen years old and I was at the movies on a Friday night with my parents!

Kill me now.

My only hope was that I wouldn't run into anybody I knew, so I tried to make myself as inconspicuous as possible and prayed no one would notice me or see me or even just look my way. I'm easy enough to miss—I'm on the short side with dark hair that's somewhere between wavy and straight but is more unruly than anything else. My eyes and hair are dark brown, and I have skin the color of coconut cream. My nose is by far my best feature, small and flat.

Unfortunately, even if there's nothing remarkable about me, it was still kind of hard to hide since I was wearing the same extremely loud red-and-gold, puffy San Francisco 49ers football jacket as the three other people in my family.

We all owned the same jacket because last month when we went on a family outing to Fisherman's Wharf we were freezing even though it was 70 degrees out. There was a sidewalk sale of these discounted 49ers jackets and we all got one. Mine says STEVE YOUNG on the back.

I heard one girl snicker. "What are they, like, superfans or something?" It's so ironic since we don't even watch football.

I took off my jacket and stuffed it under my arm. Pretty useless move, since Mom and Dad and my five-year-old sister, Brittany, still had theirs on, and as much as I wanted to distance myself from the family group per se, it's not like I could pretend I was there with anyone else. I didn't really fit in with the goths behind us or the hoochies in the miniskirts and platform heels in front of us, either.

Please God, I thought, *just don't let me see anyone I know. Please don't let anyone from Grosvernor be here tonight. Please please please. Please don't let anyone I know find out I have nothing better to do on a Friday night than see a movie with my parents.*

There is no God. The minute they finally let us inside, I practically tripped in front of none other than Whitney Bertoccini, Trish Santa Anna, and Georgia Wilson, the three most popular girls in my class. They were all wearing the same black wool coats, V-necked cashmere sweaters, hip-slung jeans, and clogs, with pastel Nokias surgically attached to their ears. Ugh.

They took seats in front of these really cute guys and started being really loud to get their attention. The guys then threw popcorn at them and Whitney turned around to yell at them to stop, but you could tell she really liked it.

I think Whitney might have seen me when she turned, but just in time I quickly ducked behind the gargantuan Coke cup that my dad bought. Dad always buys one of the largest size drinks because he and Mom bring plastic cups so we can all share the giant one instead of buying two medium ones and using four straws like everyone else in the world. The cups are too small to fit in the gigantic cup holders so we have to put them on our laps and be careful not to spill them, which inevitably happens anyway.

But that's not even the worst part. Mom never lets us buy popcorn at the movies. Ever. She microwaves a bag at home, then puts it in small plastic bags that she hands out when we get to the theater. The popcorn is all cold and there's no butter or salt on it. Mom has to be really loud about it, too—her voice is kind of high and excitable and she gets all "Vicenza, do you have your pop-corn? Do you want another bag, *iha*? There's lots more!" At least she didn't offer any to our neighbors. The last time she did that, I pretended I didn't know who the crazy lady was.

When I grow up and have lots of money the first thing I'm

going to do is go to the movies and buy the biggest tub of popcorn, put tons of butter and salt on it, and eat it all by myself.

Sitting there waiting for the movie to begin, I felt as if everyone was staring at us like we were freaks, with our plastic mini-cups of Coke and Ziploc bags of stale homemade popcorn.

I was glad Whitney and all those guys were too busy pelting each other with jujubes to even notice me. Whitney and her friends were really boisterous. But when the movie started no one told them to shut up because basically everyone in the theater was doing the same thing—yelling at the screen and blowing straw wrappers at each other. Except for my family. We were all sitting quietly in the back. Then Mom started making these hrrumppphing and tsk-tsk sounds every time someone in the theater laughed really loudly, which Whitney and her friends did a lot, even when there was nothing funny going on.

And Dad, who can never follow the plots of movies (he had to see *Pearl Harbor* five times until he understood what was happening—and his grandfather was in the war, hello), kept asking "What did he say?" and "Why is she pretending not to know him?" and "Who made the bet again?" in a really loud whisper. Mom tried shushing him, but I always feel bad and so I explained as much as I could. "He said he wants to know if they can still be friends. Because she's in disguise, Dad. There's no bet, Dad, he's just confused."

Finally Mom got really annoyed at the "rowdy" teenagers in front. To my complete and utter horror, she actually left her seat and complained to the manager about them. An usher came with a flashlight and told them to shut up. I just sank down lower in my seat. I hope they never find out it was my parents who got them shushed.

Not so bad, right? Nothing too awful happened, right? WRONG. I haven't gotten to the stomach-churning, awful, truly horrifying part yet. JUST WAIT.

As we were leaving, I noticed that Whitney, Georgia, and Trish were by the entrance, and they were still hanging out with the jujube-throwing guys. Which struck me as odd since Whitney supposedly has a major boyfriend who goes to Stevenson down in Carmel, but whatever. What do I know about the lifestyle of a popular girl?

Dad went to get the van, and Mom and Brittany and I had to wait in front of the theater for him. I was, like, praying that Whitney and all them would leave before my dad drove up in our van.

It wouldn't be that bad if Dad drove an SUV or a BMW like everyone else's dad at school, but Dad drives this van. It's not a Jeep or a truck (which might get us some cool points). No. It's a *van*. An old, rusted Dodge Ram with a gigantic dent in the middle. It's the ugliest van in the world. It's tan. With brown trim. It's a tan van. And there's no missing it because it's an elephant. It seats, like, fifteen people. Dad's even thinking of running an airport shuttle business with it.

The kicker is that the previous owner put a sticker in the back window that says VANS A-ROCKIN' DON'T COME A-KNOCKIN'. Mom and Dad are so square they don't even know what it means. Anyway, Whitney and her friends were all talking about some party they were headed to, and I just kind of slunk back next to the door, hoping they wouldn't see me.

Mom was, like, "Good movie, huh?"

And I was all, yeah, whatever. I just wanted the evening to end. Not even the happiest Hollywood ending could cheer me up by then.

Then the strangest thing happened. I looked up and accidentally caught Whitney's eye and she totally smiled at me. At me! I got this funny feeling that she actually liked me instead of thinking I'm some sort of weirdo. Whitney and I have English together and once she read over my shoulder when she forgot her copy of *Macbeth*. Maybe she thinks I'm nice. Maybe she even thinks my 49ers puffy jacket is cute, because she wears this ratty white goose-down one to school with all these ski-lift tags hanging from the sleeve that everyone thinks is so cool.

And then she waved at me. With both hands! All I could think was *This is it! She's going to invite me to the party! And we're all going to start hanging out and going to the mall and maybe even sitting together at lunch!* And I was, like, pinching myself. She was WAV-ING and SMILING and SAYING HI. So I waved and smiled and said hi back.

Then she kind of motioned for me to go over to where she was.

I felt as if I was dreaming. I couldn't believe it. Whitney Bertoccini had decided I was cool enough to hang with her because—let's face it—being at the movies on a Friday night is a good indication of a late curfew. Maybe she thought my parents were my friends. My mom looks really young—people always ask if she's my sister or something. Usually I really hate that because *how weird*, but Friday night I thought, yeah, *they think I'm just hanging out with a couple of college kids, totally. Why not?*

So I stuck my hands in my puffy 49ers jacket and I walked really casually toward the group. I smiled at the three girls (I was too nervous to even look at the boys, although I noticed one of them is really cute and looks kind of like Tobey Maguire), but they all just looked at me vacantly.

I didn't know what to do, so I just blurted, "Uh, hi, guys."

The blank looks continued. This went on for what seemed like ages. We were just staring at each other. I began to worry.

Then Georgia said, "Oh, there she is!"

So I turned around to look where she was pointing.

It turned out they were all waving and smiling and cooing over my little sister, BRITTANY.

Brit walked over, and Whitney asked her, "You're in kindergarten with my sister Pemberton, right? You're so cute! What are you doing out on Friday night? Do you have a date?"

Brittany laughed and said no, and they all petted her. Whitney gave her the last of her jujubes, and with a smile Brit scampered back to Mom's side.

I was still standing in front of them. I didn't know what to do. It was like I was completely invisible. Maybe I don't really exist. Maybe I'm just a figment of my own imagination. My legs were rooted to the spot. I was absolutely frozen. I wished I could just disappear.

Finally, after the longest, awkwardest pause of my awkward life, they noticed me.

"Hey," Whitney said. She handed me her empty, crumpled popcorn bag. "Could you throw this away?"

"Oh. Sure," I responded. And I took her garbage and walked back to where Mom and Brittany were standing next to the trash can, but I couldn't even throw it away because I was in TOTAL SHOCK.

"Do you know those girls?" Mom asked.

I shook my head. "Nope." I was utterly hopeless. I knew I'd NEVER be able to face them on Monday.

"I do," Brittany chirped, her face full of Whitney's jujubes. "They're really nice."

Even my five-year-old sister is more popular than I am.

FROM: queen_vee@aol.com
TO: amparo.dellarosa@info.ph.com
SENT: Sunday, October 4, 8:30 AM
SUBJECT: awesome wkend!

Peaches!

How are you, *bruha*? You probably think I'm a witch, too, for only writing now! I'm so sorry. I've been super busy . . . went to the movies on Friday with my best friend, Whitney, and a bunch of peeps and I met this total hottie who was totally checking me out! He looks exactly like Tobey Maguire—I know I say that about every guy I crush on, but this time it's true, I swear!

Anyway, gotta run. We're late for church and Dad's having an aneurysm.

XXOOO,

V

PS—My mom says hi to your mom and wants to know if she can send her that special nipper that they get from Chinatown. Mom can't find the same one here as in Manila and says her cuticles are atrosh!

2

Fortunately for Some Girls, Some Cute Boys Can't Drive

THERE ARE ONLY a few ways to meet boys at an all-girls school like Grosvernor: you are so incredibly popular that boys from other schools immediately flock to you, you're so incredibly talented that you are chosen to play Claire Danes in the interschool production of Baz Luhrmann's *Romeo and Juliet*, you are incredibly lucky and have a cool older brother with cute friends, or last, and certainly the very least, you can join the Spirit Club.

Since everything else was completely out of the question, on Monday, after the final bell rang, I patiently stood in line to board a yellow school bus, clutching a bedraggled, homemade, Crayola-and-Magic-Marker banner that shrieked GO WILD-CATS!!!! with a crudely drawn lion on it (since I had no idea what a wildcat actually looks like). I could have spent my time cropping pictures on an iMac and writing five-hundred-word features on Teachers of the Week for the *Daily Grosvernorian*, writing speeches about the new world order for Model United Nations, or even painting background scenery for the Drama Club. But instead I opted for a ride on the Spirit bus, which transported its members to the marina downtown for the alleged purpose of cheering on the Gros Grasshoppers as they lost yet another game of field hockey to the St. Rose Salamanders.

But let's get real. The Montclair Academy Wildcats—from the all-boys school down the hill and the three-time conference champ of the N.P.P.S.L.L. (The North Pacific Private School Lacrosse League, otherwise known as Nipple)—and their weekly lacrosse game were the *real* attraction. Several freshmen and sophomores as well as a good number of upperclassmen were already lined up in front, wearing Montclair Academy T-shirts and waving orange-and-blue banners similar to mine. A truly fine show of school spirit all around—just not for our school.

While waiting for the bus, I noticed Whitney, Georgia, and Trish sitting on the front steps, fiddling with their hair and cosmetic cases. I couldn't help but overhear what they were saying.

"Do you think he'll show?" Trish asked.

"Well, he called last night and said he would," Whitney said. "If he bails, we can always hit Stonestown." Trish and Georgia suppressed anxious sighs.

I wondered whom they were talking about. If a boy ever called me—which probably would never happen in my lifetime—I would probably get so flustered I would end up hanging up on him immediately. Not that one would ever call, of course. I'm convinced I'll never have a boyfriend. It's so unfair. Even Peaches, my best friend from Manila, has one, and she's not allowed to date until *college*.

"But we go to the mall all the time," Trish complained.

"So?" Whitney asked in a slightly annoyed tone that made Trish immediately back off. Trish is a new addition to Whitney's inner circle and assumes a perpetual expression of amazement at being promoted into the In group. This much I learned from the "lifers"—girls who had been at Grosvernor since kindergarten and who had been obsessing over Whitney for decades, marking how she wore her cranberry blazer, how high she rolled up her uniform skirt, and how slouchy she pushed down her socks.

Recently, Whitney had begun wearing black tights instead of socks, plain white T-shirts instead of regulation oxford button-downs, and a hooded cranberry sweatshirt instead of a proper sweater. The administration was not pleased, since it meant half the freshman population was in detention every day for being out of uniform. I had yet to see Whitney detained for longer than five minutes, however, since she charmed her way out of every situation with a toss of her blond ponytail.

"Omigod! It's like three twenty! Where is he? We're going to be late!" Whitney said, holding up her arm and frowning at her Cartier tank watch that glinted in the sun. I nervously twiddled with the frayed strap of the Fossil watch my mom had bought me in Hong Kong for my thirteenth birthday.

"We could always take the Spirit bus!" Georgia shrieked.

"You *cannot* be serious!" Whitney said, crinkling her nose. The three of them dissolved into another round of giggles.

It was so easy for them—they were the type of girls who probably received a dozen valentines on February fourteenth ever since the third grade. Not to be petty, but they weren't even that pretty. Oh, I guess Whitney is—she has the kind of hair and skin that glows and the kind of figure (long, slender limbs, small waist) that every girl envies. But Georgia is slightly cross-eyed, and Trish's ears stick out. I'd noticed Trish looked Asian but had a Spanish last name. "Are you Filipino?" I'd inquired on the first day of school. "Yes" she'd said and turned away. Apart from the two Chinese girls who spent every second together in the computer lab, Trish was the only other Asian girl in my class. But so much for that.

I had one foot on the step of the bus when a silver BMW convertible powered up the hill and pulled up in front of the school behind the bus. The car was filled with the same boys from the movie theater. Several lacrosse sticks were piled vertically on the backseat.

"They're heeere!" Trish squealed. "Omigod! Do I have lipstick on my teeth?"

Georgia demanded, "Hand me my hairbrush!"

"Quick! I need to blot with a tissue!" The two of them disappeared in a cloud of hair spray and a frenzy of makeup application. Only Whitney was nonchalant, picking at her cuticles as if she didn't have a care in the world.

They each straightened up as the car parallel parked in front of them. "Hey, guys," the girls cooed.

Whitney stood up and walked toward the car, slinging her Kate Spade messenger bag over one shoulder. "Cute car," she said.

The driver, a cutie who looked vaguely familiar, winked at her. "Nice T-shirts," he said. One of the boys climbed out and opened the door to let the girls inside.

"Shotgun!" Whitney called, before sliding in the front seat. Georgia and Trish squeezed into the back with what looked like the rest of the lacrosse team. They pulled out just as a red motor scooter shot out of a hidden driveway.

The BMW swerved to the side to miss the scooter. "Watch out!" someone yelled, as the driver slammed on the brakes and the car skidded for a few feet, clipping the scooter and plowing through the crowd in front of the bus. Girls screamed as backpacks and banners and pom-poms flew everywhere. I was pushed backward, and fell on top of the girl who'd been driving the scooter. We were the only ones hit. She lay sprawled next to me, her legs still wrapped around the bike. I was dazed and disoriented but miraculously unhurt, save my bloody palms and knees, which had scraped the sidewalk.

"Jesus! Are you guys okay?"

I blinked and almost fainted again when I saw the concerned face of Tobey Maguire looking down at me. Oh. My. God. Was I dreaming?

"Yeah, I think so," I said, not knowing if it was true but feeling the need to reassure him nonetheless.

The girl and I disentangled ourselves from each other. I was still shaking, but it wasn't from the accident. I realized it wasn't Tobey himself but the guy I'd seen at the movie theater Friday night. AND HE WAS GORGEOUS!!! He kneeled down next to us and helped my fellow victim to her feet.

"*MERDE!*" she said, taking off her helmet and shaking her hair, which was cut short in a pixie. She wore cat's-eye glasses that gave her a cosmopolitan air. I recognized her as the French girl who'd just started at Gros. Whitney and her friends had immediately dubbed her Eurotrash because she wore a purple leather jacket with "Cavalli" scripted on the back instead of Patagonia fleece hoodies like everyone else.

"Sorry about that," he told her.

"Next time, please observe where you are going!" she scolded, assessing the damage to her vehicle and dusting gravel off her jacket. She propped up the scooter and inspected it carefully. A torrent of foreign words exploded from her lips when she noticed the mirror was cracked.

"Oh, man, that sucks," he said, peering at it. "Listen, tell me your name and your phone number and I'll pay for it. My insurance will cover it."

She looked up at him skeptically and shrugged. "Oh well, it's not a bother. It is also my fault. I should have been more the vigilance."

"No, seriously, I insist. I feel terrible," he said.

I was still on the sidewalk, and slowly picked myself up, marveling at the torn jeans she wore under her uniform. They looked just like the ones Hilarie was wearing on *TRL* the other day.

"Listen, let me give you my number. Call and tell me how much I owe you, okay?" he said, looking around for a piece of paper or a pen.

He spotted me still holding my GO WILDCATS!!!! banner. "Can I tear a piece off?"

"Um, sure," I said, as he tore off a small wedge.

I handed him a pen from my backpack, which had miraculously survived the collision intact.

"Thanks." He nodded, scribbling his name. I peered over his shoulder. Claude Caligari! (How cute a name is that?) And his phone number (quickly committed to memory). He handed her the paper and she folded and stuffed it into her jacket pocket.

"DUDE! WE'VE GOTS TO GO! GAME TIME!" A loud voice yelled. The posse in the convertible started honking the horn, and I could see Whitney looking pissed as she peered through the windshield.

"All right, already! You guys are okay, right?" he asked again. "Seriously, I feel terrible," he said, patting my shoulder.

I nodded. "I'm fine, really." A popular boy touched me! I'm never going to wash this blazer ever again!

"See you guys at the game?"

"Sure." I smiled. The French girl climbed back on her scooter and didn't seem to notice him.

He hurried back to the car, taking long, loping strides. I watched as he fired up the engine and drove off slowly, waving to us as he turned the corner. Only then did I realize the Spirit bus had also left. "Oh no!" I said, as the yellow school bus lumbered down the hill. I started to run after it, but my knees were shaky, and my palms were starting to hurt. I didn't notice until then that little bits of gravel were embedded in my skin.

"You're not going anywhere. Vi-chen-za, right?" the French girl asked.

"Uh-huh," I said, amazed that she pronounced my name correctly. My parents named me after the city in the Veneto in

Italy, where they honeymooned, and I had yet to meet anyone who said it correctly. I'd learned to answer to "Vi-jen-za," "Vi-sen-za," or "Vi-ken-za." In Manila, they had skipped the issue completely by calling me "V."

"I'm Isobel Saint-Pierre," she said, smiling. "I think maybe we should both go to the clinic."

We hobbled back together to the large white Georgian-style mansion that housed the upper form, her scooter rolling silently between us.

"Cool Vespa," I said, patting the seat.

"Thanks." Isobel smiled.

"But don't you have to be sixteen to drive one?"

"Yes, but I have diplomatic immunity," she said airily.

"Really?"

"Well, I think so. I'm a French citizen. Anyway, I'm fourteen-and-a-half. That should count, shouldn't it?"

I didn't think it did, but I didn't want to tell her that.

"You're from France?"

"Paris. But Papa moves a lot for work. He is a university pro-fessor. We were in New York last year. They wouldn't let me have a scooter there, since they were too frightened the traffic would kill me. But they said I could have one in San Francisco, even if it's a little crazy getting up and down the hills."

I noticed a Spider-Man sticker on her book bag. "Oh my god,

are you into Tobey Maguire, too?" I asked, showing her the same sticker on my three-ring binder.

"He is a god!" She laughed.

Isobel left her scooter on the sidewalk, and we walked through the double-height bronze doors. The elderly receptionist was closing up for the day, but she told us the clinic was still open.

Inside the great hall, a catering company was setting up for the evening. Grosvernor was a designated historical landmark, and after hours, the school was one of the most sought-after event spaces in the city. A long banquet table was laden with steaming silver buffet pans, plates, and assorted cutlery.

"Mmm, something smells delicious!" Isobel declared. She walked over to the nearest one and opened the lid. "Shrimp fritters! *Très bien!* My favorite!" she said, swiping a few with a napkin.

"Isobel!" I said, scandalized, looking around to see if any of the scurrying tuxedoed waiters or white-jacketed chefs had noticed.

"Want one?" she asked, popping another into her mouth.

I shook my head, but it was seriously tempting. I was amazed at her brazenness. My best friend back in Manila, Peaches, is just like me—neither of us would ever do anything to break the rules. We've never even jaywalked.

We tiptoed past a harried woman in a headset barking orders

and trudged up the winding marble stairs to the nurse's office on the fourth floor, Isobel still munching on the pilfered treats.

"Here," she said, and before I could protest, she brusquely placed a warm, flaky shrimp in my hand.

I was frightened—could they kick me out of school for being an accomplice to an hors d'oeuvres thief? But, on the other hand, I was kind of hungry. I nodded my thanks and devoured it whole. I wiped my sticky fingers on my skirt and followed her into the clinic.

As the nurse cleaned and bandaged our wounds, we compared schedules. I was pleased to learn that besides being in the same English class, we had lunch at the same time—G period, which meant I might have someone to eat with in the cafeteria. Lately, I'd taken to sneaking my sandwiches into the library.

"Ouch!" Isobel yelped as the nurse applied antiseptic to her scratch. I ended up with matching Band-Aids on each knee but at least my palms had stopped throbbing.

Isobel offered to drive me home, but I explained I lived in South San Francisco—and not in the Bayview or Excelsior district but in a different town altogether, forty-five minutes away, which declared itself SOUTH SAN FRANCISCO: THE INDUSTRIAL CITY in mile-high capital letters on a hill. Just like the HOLLYWOOD sign but not.

We said good-bye, and I watched her ease her scooter out and drive it slowly down the tree-lined block. When she got to the corner, she waved before disappearing down Fillmore Street. I walked up another block to take the bus.

Usually, Dad picked up Brittany and me from school, but since I was supposed to be going to the game with the Spirit Club, he had already gotten her earlier. They were both waiting for me at his office downtown, a twenty-minute ride on the Jackson Street bus. I liked meeting Dad at his office since his building was across from Market Street, where I could hang out at the Gap, Rolo's, Tower Records, and Nordstrom.

The only thing I didn't like were the pink mohawked punks who loitered around Market Street in full studded-leather-and-torn-T-shirt regalia. I was always a little afraid of them. I didn't understand what they were calling me at first, but I soon learned it wasn't very nice. They never failed to comment whenever I walked by—yelling out "FOB!" (fresh off the boat), which infuriated me since I had arrived in this country on a Boeing 747. I managed to hurry by without arousing their interest, however. Perhaps they were having an off day.

"*Anong nangyari sa iyo?*" Dad asked, when I arrived at Arambullo Import Trading. He shook his head at me when he saw the Band-Aids on my hands and knees. "*Akala ko* you were going to the game?"

"*Wala*, I fell. I missed the bus." I shrugged, walking over to greet him with a kiss on the cheek.

"You should be more careful!" he said. Dad always got angry as a way of expressing concern. When I was little, I was terrified whenever I hurt myself because Dad's wrath was so much more frightening than the pain of any cuts or scrapes.

I dropped my book bag on the floor, where Brittany was stretched out, coloring with crayons in a book. "Hi, *Ate*," she said, without looking up. My parents insisted Brittany call me "ate" the proper title for "big sister" as customary in Filipino families.

"V, you know you can just call me V," I whispered, since I was trying to discourage the habit.

Dad's office was just big enough to hold the three of us with all of his furniture. When you opened the door, it hit the guest chair. In the middle of the room was a big black metal desk with a battered old computer he had bought at a garage sale, a phone, and an ancient fax machine. It was so old it still used the shiny paper that spooled through in a continuous sheet that you had to rip off at the top. There was a filing cabinet wedged behind the desk on which Mom had placed a goldfish bowl with one lone goldfish. "For luck!" she said, explaining a Chinese superstition. A ceramic kitten with its paw sticking up stood guard on top of the minifridge. ("It's supposed to bring in money! Japanese good luck charm!") There was a pineapple-shaped ashtray and a pineapple-shaped coffee mug. (Hawaiians believed pineapples

brought prosperity.) Mom believed in adopting as many super-
stitions as she could—you never know which one will work, she
always said. My dad ran an import-export business, to bring
Philippine products to American sellers and vice versa. So far,
despite the numerous lucky charms, he'd had absolutely no luck.

In Manila, my parents had owned one of the nicest restaurants in Makati, and my dad had been an investment banker who
owned his own company, Arambullo Investments. He had the
biggest office in the building on the top floor, with floor-to-
ceiling windows and white shag carpeting. He had three secre-
taries: one to take calls, one to file, and another just to order
Christmas gifts. The few times I'd visited my dad at his office, I
was always amazed—everyone, from the bank tellers to the mes-
sengers to the receptionists and VP's seemed to know who I was.
"Mr. Arambullo's kid, right?" "Oh, the daughter of the Big
Boss!" Mom said that everyone at the office was scared of my
dad, so I liked marching in, bursting in on his meetings or while
he was on the phone or with a guest. Dad would shush me, but
he would never ask me to leave. Instead, I would sit on one of
the black leather couches next to the conference table and look
out at the view or else admire the framed pictures of lions and
waterfalls that I'd drawn which were his office's sole decoration.

"Can I go to Nordstrom?" I asked.

"No, I'm done here," Dad said, pulling out his briefcase. He placed a few file folders inside. "Bri-tta-ny, pack up *na*."

My sister nodded and started carefully putting away her things. Brittany is very particular about her stuff. We once had a huge fight when I tore a piece of paper from her notebook and left the little frayed edges on the ring. Unlike me, she hates to make a mess.

I glanced at paper on the top of my dad's desk. It was a memo about Philippine lumber being a great source of wood for pencils and rulers. "Ask about our low prices and international delivery." In the three months we'd lived here, he'd only been able to sell one order of pencils and one order of rulers to a school-supply company in Minnesota.

Brittany and I waited in the dim hallway while Dad locked up his office. He always wore a suit and a tie to work, even though he was the company's sole employee. He looked tired and drained. His suit jacket was frayed at the edges. According to my parents, moving to America was supposed to be our "new adventure"—halfway between an exciting journey and a long-term vacation. We never really talked about home, and never once did anybody in my family ever mention how much they would like to go back there. Or how much we missed it. Not only was I homesick for my friends and our extended family but I also longed for our old life. But my parents made it clear that it wasn't an option, although I still didn't really understand why not.

In any case, leaving Manila did seem pretty final. My mom cried when we sold our house, and I'd sat quietly while neighbors and strangers appraised our things and put bids on them— my parents' wedding china and silver, the custom-made carved napa-wood coffee table, the Viking range.

On the way out, like he always does, Dad stopped by Gino's deli to buy a lottery ticket. He always plays the same numbers: 7, 29, 22, and 6—our birthdays. Dad was inspired by a Filipino man he knew who won the lottery. *Mang* Pedro used to be our gardener in Manila until he moved to Texas. After he hit the fifty-million-dollar jackpot, his grown children immigrated to America to be with him. When they arrived at the airport, they showed the INS officer the newspaper clipping of their father holding up the humongous check, to prove that they could afford to live here. True story. Dad still thinks this could happen to us.

Alfonse, who owns Gino's deli, solemnly wished us good luck after handing Dad his daily lottery ticket, and the three of us walked to the garage under the building where the van was parked.

On the way home, I thought about my dad and the lottery obsession. He was so sure we would hit the jackpot one day. Maybe delusion ran in the family, because my knees still ached from almost being run over, but all I could think about was how

Claude's hand had pressed gently on my shoulder. If he hadn't almost killed me, we would never have met. Claude Caligari—I savored the syllables in my head. *He has the nicest eyes*, I thought. And he had really looked concerned about my welfare, not just scared that he might get in trouble or anything.

We drove by the marina before we hit the freeway. In the distance, I could see boys in brightly colored orange-and-blue jerseys shouldering their sticks and walking off the field. A few girls in Gros uniforms were walking toward the dependable yellow school bus parked on the corner. I squinted, but I couldn't see a silver convertible anywhere.

The game was over. I wondered who won.

FROM: queen_vee@aol.com
TO: amparo.dellarosa@info.ph.com
SENT: Monday, October 5, 9:30 PM
SUBJECT: lacrosse queen

Guess who just called? Claude Caligari—the cute guy from the movies! (BTW, he really does look like Tobey—except he has blue eyes and blond hair, but other than that—twins, *talaga*!) Omigod, he has the cutest voice on the phone. This afternoon he picked me up from school so I could watch him play lacrosse. (He's the Montclair Academy team captain!) The game was so exciting—St. Augustus was in the lead, 1–0 for four quarters, but at the last minute, he scored two goals!! Lacrosse is kind of like soccer meets jai alai (except no betting). After the game, we went to get burgers at Mel's Diner with the gang, then he drove everyone home.

That is so great about you and Rufi! He sounds adorable. Are you guys officially a couple now? What about your parents? Are you scared they'll find out?

Hey, we heard about the bomb on the Lovebus— *nakakatakot*! My parents were so worried about everyone back home, but I was like, Mom, hello, nobody we know in Manila takes public transportation!

xxoo, V

3

Even in English Class, Everything is in French

THE NEXT MORNING, rooting through the mail on the kitchen counter for the newest Delia's catalog, I found a thick, ivory-colored envelope. It looked expensive and special, and if you held it up to the light, you could spy a watermark with the Grosvernor crest. It had no place in our Formica kitchen, where the linoleum was peeling off in strips and there were so many cracks that no matter how hard my mother scrubbed, it always looked dirty.

Ugh. I knew what it contained. I put it in the trash without opening it and left for school.

I walked in late for my first class, and I'd even missed homeroom, since Brittany couldn't find her Hello Kitty socks that morning and caused a terrific stink. Brit can be a real brat sometimes, and my parents don't even mind. She gets away with everything because she's the baby—it's so unfair. I was especially annoyed because I hated walking in late, especially for English, which I dreaded even if it was my favorite subject. Unlike all the other classrooms, with normal individual desks and chairs, the English classroom only had a large round table in the middle. Everyone saved seats for their friends—but nobody ever saved me a seat, so I always had to sit in the dunce chair next to Dr. Avilla, who was nice enough, but what a loser move to actually have to sit next to the *teacher*.

Saving seats was a big deal at Gros. If no one saved you a seat, it was the surest sign you were nobody. Whitney, Georgia, and Trish always made a big deal of sitting next to each other. Once, I made the mistake of taking Whitney's seat (I didn't notice Trish's notebook on it), so Whitney had to sit in the very front, and she complained about it the whole time, saying she was allergic to blackboard chalk.

But when I walked in, I found Isobel, the French girl, waving to me from the far side of the conference table. "Vicenza! *Reposez-vous ici!*" She had taken the best seats in the house—next to the window. She shifted her books off the chair next to her so I could sit down.

"Thanks," I whispered, so happy that I couldn't stop my cheeks from turning pink.

She nodded. *"Rien."*

As Dr. Avilla droned on about *The Old Man and the Sea*, she scribbled notes to me in the margins of her notebook. I felt hesitant at first (this was definitely against the rules), but soon I found I was writing back as fast as I could.

In this way I discovered Isobel was just like me: she had moved to the States that summer, adored Mexican food, liked to quote lines from *Good Will Hunting* ("so inspirational"), downloaded dance remixes of cheesy pop songs on Kazaa, and loathed Whitney Bertoccini upon meeting her for the first time.

We were interrupted when Dr. Avilla asked Isobel to read from last night's homework and she got a lecture on how atrocious her English was. He said it was absolutely criminal that a fourteen-year-old girl, bilingual as she was, had such a poor grasp of English grammar. Isobel argued that she was fluent in French, and since French was a Romance language, it was infinitely superior and truly the language of the civilized world, while English was derived from the bastard tongue of barbarians. Strangely enough, he didn't take too kindly to her opinions.

Avilla the Hun! she wrote in my notebook margin.

I suppressed a giggle.

To my surprise, Isobel didn't seem to care that people snickered about her purple jacket. She walked around Gros totally oblivious to the fact that despite the school uniform she didn't look like anybody else. It didn't bother her one bit. She sang aloud off key to her iPod, wore her knee socks pulled all the way up (everyone else scrunched theirs down, as was the current fashion), and joked around in rapid French with the intimidating French mistress, Mademoiselle Fraley, in the hallways as if "Mamselle" were just a classmate. One day she walked in with a bright pink streak in her hair, and when the dean asked her to explain, she said she'd tried to fix it but she was worried if she dyed it again it would turn green.

Isobel's PeeChee folders, textbooks, and three-ring binder were totally graffitied with song lyrics and drawings. Her locker was a mess of *CosmoGirl* posters and Evanescence stickers. She wasn't anything like Peaches back home, who was neat to the point of obsession. But they did have something in common. Both of them had the same laugh. Like Peaches, Isobel snorted when she laughed—and not with small, quick bursts either but with loud, embarrassing Mr. Snuffleupagus grunts—*hrog, hrog, hrog*—which made the other girls shrink back in distaste. When Isobel found something funny, she couldn't help herself. Her shoulders shook, and her hands waved in front of her belly as she hiccupped and snorted.

A week after Claude almost killed both of us with his car, we were walking out of English, talking animatedly about the pros and cons of dating Ben Affleck versus Matt Damon (Isobel was in the Ben camp and I passionately argued that someone who would make fun of his ex-girlfriend on *SNL* probably wouldn't make such a good catch) when Dr. Avilla asked if we could stay behind. I thought for sure we were in trouble. We had been reckless, the notes flying back and forth on our notebooks crammed with caricatures and insults, only paying the least bit of attention to the lesson at hand.

"I'm going to have to separate you two," Dr. Avilla said sternly.

We were definitely in trouble. My parents would kill me. I'd never gotten in trouble in my life.

"What do you mean, Dr. A?" Isobel asked with a grin. She was fearless.

Dr. Avilla shook his head. "Can I borrow Vicenza for a minute?" he asked.

"Oui." She shrugged.

"See you at the caf?" I asked.

She nodded as she walked away.

It was then that I noticed Dr. Avilla was holding up an essay I had written last week about Camus' *The Stranger*. Above my name was a red letter A scrawled inside a circle.

"Vicenza, how long have you been in this country?" he asked.

"Um, three months," I replied, a little wary.

"That's amazing. And you learned English so quickly? You

don't even have an accent!"

"Oh, no, actually, we speak English in Manila," I said, explaining something people in the States didn't seem to understand. "Everything is taught in English—science, social studies, math. Tagalog is like a second language."

"Oh. I'm sorry, I didn't know that." He smiled. "For a minute there, I thought you were a prodigy or a genius," he joked.

"I wanted to tell you, you're wasted here." He motioned to the empty room. "I'm booting you up to the honors class. This essay is even better than any my honors students have produced this year."

"Really?"

Honors English was, well, an honor. They went on field trips to see movies at the art-house cinema in the Haight and Dr. Avilla took them to readings and book signings. There was a two-week summer trip to England to go see the Poet's Corner and where Shakespeare lived.

I thanked Dr. Avilla profusely. At lunchtime, I picked up my lunch from my locker and walked to the belvedere, a marbled room that had been renovated to accommodate the Gros cafeteria. I found Isobel sitting at a corner table under a large, pink-and-silver poster that blared GET YOUR TICKETS TO THE SOIRÉE D'HIVER NOW!!! JOIN THE SOCIAL CLUB TO PLAN THE YEAR'S BEST DANCE!!!

"Yuck. What a waste of time," I said, pointing to the incriminating sign.

"So *stupide*," Isobel agreed, as she nibbled on her steak frites. She had her lunch delivered every day from a French bistro on Fillmore Street. She motioned at the crisp, golden fries, and I marveled that Isobel didn't seem to follow any of those trendy low-carb diets that everyone else in class followed religiously.

I bit into my microwaved burrito. Mom had just discovered the joys of the frozen food aisle at Safeway. In Manila, we had wet and dry markets, where everything was so fresh, the fish flipped out of baskets and the tomatoes were still on the vine, and there were buckets of fresh crabs and giant prawns, juicy sweet mangos and purple guavas.

Supermarkets were a constant source of amazement for my family. A trip to the grocery store was like discovering a new continent—and we couldn't believe how cold it was. Brittany had to wear two jackets and a sweater when we went to Safeway. "This is a great and strange land," my dad concluded, after surveying the overwhelming amount of choices in the cheese aisle: lowfat, nonfat, fat-free, reduced cholesterol, no carbohydrates, low sodium, or calcium added. Of course, we loaded up the cart with Twinkies and Chips Ahoy cookies, which were criminally expensive at the PX Import Shop back in Manila but dirt cheap at Safeway. After six weeks, the four of us each gained fifteen pounds. I was still trying to lose ten of mine.

I opened a granola bar (which I'd had to beg Mom to buy— the concept of health food was anathema to a Filipino palate) and ignored the cackling from Whitney's table.

"So, you're not going to the Soirée?" I asked Isobel, relieved.

"I've been to real nightclubs in Manhattan. Why do I care about some silly dance? *C'est un jeu d'enfants. Pas d'importance.*"

I guess that meant she didn't have a date either, but her indifference was convincing. It was probably just her accent, which made everything she said sound so worldly and sophisticated. She said Claude never even called about replacing the mirror, like a "typical American."

To change the subject, I told her how I'd been bumped up to Honors English.

"So you're not in my class anymore?" Isobel asked, eyes wide.

In my excitement, I had completely forgotten what it would mean. No more secret notes, no more saved seats.

Sigh.

FROM: queen_vee@aol.com

TO: amparo.dellarosa@info.ph.com

SENT: Friday, October 16, 8:35 PM

SUBJECT: RE: how are you??

Hi, Peach—

School is good so far. Classes are really easy, except for geometry, which is a complete waste of time. But the good news is that I got transferred to Honors English. Still, it's bittersweet because all my friends are in regular. Whitney was really sad about it. She says hi, by the way.

Love,

V

4
Saturdays at America's Favorite Store

THIS CAME FOR you last week," Mom said, pushing a familiar-looking envelope toward me as we wolfed down our breakfast of maple-sugar doughnuts and coffee. It was eight in the morning on Saturday, and we had to get to work by nine, in order to set up before everyone arrived.

"I found it in the trash and forgot to give it to you," she explained, wiping confectioner's sugar from the corners of her mouth. "Daddy must have made a mistake."

I shrugged. I hadn't even bothered to open the envelope. I already knew what it contained.

"Open it," she urged.

I ignored her and helped myself to another doughnut and began chewing it ferociously. It was our favorite breakfast, and one I was allowed as a special treat on Saturdays since I had to work all day with Mom at our cafeteria. On school days, I usually had oatmeal or toast.

Seeing that I was determined to leave the envelope where it lay, she picked it up and carefully slit the edge with a letter opener. She pulled out a thick, embossed card with gold trim covered in pale ivory tissue. "Oh, how nice!" she exclaimed, and read aloud the words that were written in curlicue calligraphy:

Miss Maria Vicenza Esmeralda Rodriguez Arambullo
and Escort
are cordially invited to attend the
Montclair Academy–Grosvenor School for Girls
Annual Soirée d'Hiver
December the Nineteenth
The Top of the Mark Hotel, 8 P.M.
$90 each, $150 per couple
Black Tie

I made a face. "It's just a stupid dance."

"*Bakit? Ayaw mo pumunta?*"

"No, I don't want to go."

"But you love to dance!" she argued, taking another doughnut.

"It's not like I have anyone to go with."

"*Aba!* What are you talking about? There's Freddie!" she said indignantly.

UGH.

Freddie.

No way.

I was NOT taking Mom's friend from church's dorky son Freddie Dalugdugan to the Soirée.

It's bad enough that Freddie's real name is John Fitzgerald Kennedy Junior Dalugdugan. Then again, I have a cousin named Jesse James Arambullo and an uncle named Pat Boone del Rosario. Filipinos are funny about names.

Freddie is a total pain. He's an enginerd. I guess I should thank him for teaching me how to download movies from the Internet, but still. He's zitty and scrawny and weighs ninety pounds dripping wet. He wears thick, Coke-bottle glasses and a satin baseball jacket with the Olympic logo that reads SYDNEY 2000 on the back. I'm three inches taller than him, and I'm 5 foot 4!

Freddie is a senior at Montclair and has made the front cover of *The Filipino Reporter*'s Bay Area edition three times: first when he was a National Merit Scholar, second when he won first place in the Westinghouse Science Fair, and third when he scored a perfect 1,600 on his SATs. He'll probably have his entire life and career recorded in that publication. Freddie gets a job at NASA! Freddie gets married to Miss

Philippines-USA! Freddie runs for mayor of Daly City!

I didn't dislike Freddie, but there was no way I was showing up at some la-di-da school ball at the Top of the Mark with him on my arm. I'd rather stay home.

Unfortunately, Mom felt differently.

"You know," she said, placing the card back in the envelope, "you should really try harder to fit in. Can't you do that for Daddy and me?"

I stared down at the floor and said nothing, tearing the napkin I held under the table into a million pieces. How could I explain what school was like to my mom? They were so proud that I had been accepted into Gros with an academic scholarship. But they had NO IDEA what my life was like. They never even noticed how pathetic it was that I spent every weekend at home with them and that I didn't have any friends who ever called me at home or on the cell phone they bought me because the family plan was cheap. They had already warned me that I wasn't allowed to date until I was fifteen. Boy, they sure had nothing to worry about.

"I know it's been hard on you, V. I know you miss your friends back home. But this is home now. I think the dance might be fun. Isn't everyone going?"

Was she kidding?

It was the only thing girls in my class talked about all week.

Who they were taking (boys from Montclair, of course), what they were wearing (slinky halter dresses from BCBG), where they would go afterward (Margy McCarthy's beach house in Marin).

The pathetic thing was, I agreed with my mother. I did want to fit in. I did want to go to the dance. More than anything in the world. But I would never, never, never admit it to anybody. NEVER. Not even to my mom. I know it's really pathetic of me, but I just really wanted to go to the Soirée. I liked to dress up, I did like to dance, and a huge part of me really wanted to fit in. I just didn't think I ever would, so why should I try?

"You could wear my pearl earrings and my black pumps with the gold straps," Mom offered. "And, look, they're opening a Jessica McClintock factory outlet next month! Prom dresses and evening wear. We could get you a gown there," she said, showing me a clipping from yesterday's paper.

"Can we talk about this later, Mom? Aren't we going to be late?"

"*Oy, Diosko! Halika na!*" Mom looked at her watch and agreed that we should motor. On the way, we argued about the dance for a little while, and I finally agreed that I would at least think it over.

"Freddie is a really nice boy. I know he's not Mr. Universe, but if it's just a date you need . . ." Mom said, as we drove into the mall entrance. "I'm going to invite the Dalugdugans over one Sunday to watch the Niners game. Maybe you can ask him then."

I grunted a noncommittal response. My parents and the "Niners" game? Since when did we have any interest in football? Since we bought the team jackets?

The parking lot was almost completely empty when we arrived, so Mom parked right in a choice spot next to the handicapped spaces near the front. We walked through the ghostly mall, nodding to fellow proprietors who had come to open their stores.

When everything was in place, the tables sparkling with Pledge and the air scented with the appetizing smell of roasting coffee from the two machines, I erased the blackboard and wrote out the following:

WELCOME TO THE SEARS EMPLOYEES CAFETERIA!
DAILY SPECIALS, SATURDAY, OCTOBER 17:
1. Chicken and Pork Adobo
A Filipino stew with garlic, vinegar, and soy sauce. Delicious!
Served with rice and a green salad
$4.95

2. Chicken Club Sandwich
Roasted chicken breast, bacon, and avocado

on a sesame roll. Delicious!

Served with your choice of potato chips,

macaroni, or potato salad.

$3.95

3. Nachos Grande

Tortilla chips, chili, cheese, refried beans,

and jalapeño peppers. Delicious!

Served with sour cream and guacamole.

$2.95

Soup of the Day

Clam Chowder

small, $.90, large, $1.75

Served with crackers. Delicious!

HAVANADA!

"Havanada?" asked Hank, a portly, bespectacled store employee who was our first customer of the day, as he squinted at our blackboard.

I shrugged. "Havanada" was a joke of my dad's. He had written it on the board last week. I didn't get it either at first.

"Havanada?" I'd asked. "Like Canada?"

"No, no, no." Dad shook his head. "Haffa-*nigh*-day! From

Everybody Loves Raymond? Raymond goes to this Chinese restaurant and that's what the Chinese people say to him," he explained. My father was an avid fan of sitcoms and *Saturday Night Live*. He was also addicted to *Entertainment Tonight*, *Access Hollywood*, and *The National Enquirer*.

"It's nothing," I told Hank. I vowed to erase it as soon as Mom turned her back.

Hank peered at the chalkboard for a long moment, then gave me his daily breakfast order: a can of Coke, since he usually brown-bagged the rest from home.

"What are you reading?" he asked, spying a dog-eared book by the cash register while I fetched him a soda from the fridge.

"Ayn Rand."

"Huh. Never heard of her."

What a surprise. I forced myself to grin. "I guess it's no Grisham."

"That's for sure," he said, saluting me with the Coke can.

"Hello, Hank!" my mother said, walking out of the kitchen to the lunch counter. "How are you doing today?" She smiled and bowed.

"Very, very well, Marge! And you?" he asked. My mother's name is Marphindiosa, but everyone in Manila called her Didi. Here, they called her Marge. It was strange to think of my mom as a Marge. It was a name that went hand in hand with a tall blonde with a hairnet who chewed gum and wore plastic earrings. Which was completely unlike my mother, who was dark haired, petite, wore platinum jewelry, and was brought up to believe it wasn't proper for ladies to be overfamiliar with Juicy Fruit.

"Not too bad," Mom allowed.

"How's business?"

"Up and down. Win some, lose some. You know how it is."

They exchanged a few more pleasantries, my mother trying out her newly learned American idioms (she and Dad were constantly "pushing the envelope" and "thinking outside of the box"). She was smiling and nodding the whole time, as gracious as she had been when my parents owned Café Arambullo, our five-star restaurant in the middle of Makati, where she played hostess to politicians and movie stars.

The restaurant was Mom's little side project, since she had retired from her banking job when Dad founded Arambullo Investments with his best friend, Ponce Sorriano, and she was finally able to indulge in her passion for entertaining. When I was in Catholic school in Manila, our chauffeur picked me up from the convent gates at midday and drove me and a few chosen friends to the restaurant to have lunch with my mother. It was her idea to provide "lunch theater" to the business executives that frequented the place in the afternoon. I spent my lunch hours polishing off plates of steak au poivre while watching innumerable performances of *You're a Good Man, Charlie Brown*. (I still know all the lyrics.)

We watched Hank shuffle to the back of the cafeteria next to the microwave. I scowled into *The Fountainhead*. There was something so depressing about Hank—his scraggly gray hair, his deep crow's-feet, the way his horn-rimmed glasses were taped at the edges, the way his shirts strained to cover a belly that flopped over his belt like a stack of pancakes. He was almost fifty, but he worked in the stockroom with teenagers.

"You should be nicer to our customers," Mom chided. "Always this big frown. Hank is nice! At least he buys Coke from us!"

"Seventy-five cents. Big deal."

"It adds up! Look at those boys from the stockroom. They never buy from us. Never. *Palagi nalang sa* machine. Same prices! But instead of giving us the money—no, give the machine the money!" she said, wiping down the cutting boards furiously, which she did whenever she got upset.

I steeled myself for yet another lecture about my lack of proper customer care, but was thankfully spared for now since she had to chop bananas and melons for the fruit salad. A few hours later, a gaggle of bouffant-haired salesclerks from Housewares descended, with their lunch orders for tuna salad half sandwiches, fruit salads, and Diet Cokes, and for the next half hour my mother and I worked furiously. Mom slapped mustard and mayo on wheat, white, or rye bread (unless you wanted a roll, which was 50 cents extra), layering slices of roast beef, turkey, ham, and pastrami accordingly. She scooped out potato or macaroni salads for the side dishes, while I handed out sodas, worked the cash register, counted change, or added sums to several running tabs (a few of our ladies were of the tuna-salad-today-pay-you-tomorrow variety).

Mom lined up the orders with their receipts attached and it was my job to call out names once the order was ready.

"Bertha!"

"Mildred!"

"Twila!"

"Your order's ready!"

Only Mr. Bullfinch, the store manager, had the privilege of having his order personally delivered to his table (usually by me). It was one of Mom's signature ideas, a special touch—to curry favor with and allegiance from the powerful, as she had once done with the most famous patron of Café Arambullo, none other than the president of the Philippines herself. Mr. Bullfinch might not have been the supreme leader of a small, third-world country, but to us, he was just as important. He had given my parents the license to operate the cafeteria.

After the old biddies came the big-haired teenage girls from

Cosmetics and Lingerie. Sears required its employees on the sales floor to dress "professionally," which meant no denim, T-shirts, or sneakers. Most of the girls wore garish floral dresses and black tights with patent-leather heels, piled on too much makeup, and looked ten, even fifteen years older than they really were, when in reality they were only one or two years older than me. They liked to order nachos.

My parents paid me ten dollars a week to work at the cafeteria. I once pointed out to my dad that my salary amounted to a subminimum wage, which made me an illegal child laborer. Dad argued that it was a "family wage." It wasn't so bad, though, because when the cafeteria was empty—usually around eleven o'clock in the morning, right after breakfast rush and before lunch hour, I could do as I pleased. I usually spent it window-shopping at the mall, lingering over the sequin-studded tank tops at Contempo, trying on boot-cut pants at Wet Seal, wishing I could afford the leather jackets at the Limited.

When the last customer drifted off to a table carrying her tray, Mom wiped down the counter and surveyed the room with satisfaction. The cafeteria was busy, humming with the sounds of mastication and gossip. I went back to my book. Mom retreated to the kitchen to put another pot of adobo on the stove for the two o'clock round, when the burly Automotive mechanics took their break. They were always our best customers as they had heartiest appetites.

A slim boy in a red baseball cap and a black Incubus T-shirt and faded jeans entered the swinging doors. *Another stock boy headed for the Coke machine,* I thought, frowning. But when I looked up to turn the page, he was standing right in front of me.

"Hi, uh, can I get a Pepsi?" he asked.

I nodded, and he smiled, revealing two perfect rows of shining silver braces.

FROM: queen_vee@aol.com

TO: amparo.dellarosa@info.ph.com

SENT: Saturday, October 17, 3:30 PM

SUBJECT: quick question

Hi, P—

Whitney and I are at the mall, doing major damage on our moms' credit cards. (We found a free Internet station at the Burger King!) Just wanted to write a quick note and tell you what I think you should do about Rufi. . . . First of all, make sure he calls you ONLY when your parents aren't home. Second, go to the party, but make sure your *yaya* doesn't tell on you and make *sumbung*. Maybe you can bribe her with a copy of *Kislap*. Or you can get your cousin, the movie star, to sign an autograph.

xo,

V

5

Retail Therapy Salvation

OM AND I locked up at five o'clock on the dot. By four forty-five I had placed all the plastic trays with the M&M's, Snickers, Kit Kats, and Twixes away in the pantry. If a customer came in and asked for a candy bar, I would have to unlock the door; pull out the stacked, six-foot-tall cart with the perforated shelves; remove every box until I got to the right one; reach inside; and hand him the one he wanted. In other words, they were out of luck. Mom chided me on my impatience but didn't make a federal case out of it. She was as exhausted as I was.

Closing up shop meant all the Tupperware for the sandwich fixings, as well as the cutting boards, metal soup pots, and cookie pans had to be washed, dried, and put away. Mom put on extrastrength yellow rubber gloves to wash everything in scalding hot water in the industrial sinks in the back. I placed the cold cuts, vegetables, and fruits in the fridge, wiped down the counters, turned off the coffee machine, and erased the blackboard, deciding to leave "Havanada" on to please Dad.

We used an oversized grocery cart that Mom had stolen from the Costco parking lot and loaded it up with stuff we had to take home: two gallon bottles of mayonnaise and relish, boxes of beef bouillon base, and quart cans of yellow nacho cheese that couldn't fit in the fridge, as well as the twenty pounds of ground pork for homemade longanisa sausages. Mom put the day's tally ($175) into the red cookie tin (red for luck, according to the Chinese!) that we used to transport the money to the California Savings Bank the next business day.

Our cafeteria was in the back of the building, past the security room, with its banks of monitors and a holding cell (where I once saw a woman being interrogated—apparently she had been caught stuffing her bag with boxes of panty hose), past the employee bathroom (much cleaner than the public one) and the rows of open stock arranged on steel shelves. "Look how much they trust us," Mom said, marveling at the array of toasters, towel racks, and power tools we could have swiped at any moment.

I wheeled the cart out to the loading dock, where the boys from the stockroom helped shoppers put their stainless steel refrigerators and fifty-inch TVs and Kenmore dryers in the back of Ford minivans and Chevy Suburbans. The boy who'd bought a Pepsi from us earlier was rolling a washing machine on a trolley behind a family of four. He wore a tan uniform shirt over his T-shirt.

"Hi, Paul," Mom said.

I was surprised, but I shouldn't have been. Mom knew everybody's name at Sears. She made a point of it.

"Have you met my daughter Vicenza?"

"No, I mean, yeah. Hi." He flashed his braces at me.

I forced a smile, wishing I didn't blush like I did. The stock boys at Sears were nothing like the Montclair Academy preppies. Most of them had rat tails or mullets, feathered in the front and long in the back. They bought their clothes from Hot Topic instead of J.Crew and Polo. Some wore gold chains and earrings. Paul didn't look anything like the other stock boys—he didn't have any visible tattoos or body jewelry and didn't wear jeans that fell down his hips and ballooned around his legs. He had blondish-brown hair and green eyes, and he looked neat in his red baseball cap. But he didn't look anything like Tobey Maguire.

Mom said good night and the two of us walked to the parking lot. I pushed the cart out of the double doors, which Paul held open for us.

"Thanks," I said, looking down at my shoes.

"No problem." He whistled as he walked away, one hand on the trolley, the other in his pocket.

* * *

The night was warm for October, or at least, that's what I had been told. But it didn't really make a difference, I was always cold. When we'd left Manila it was ninety-eight degrees—a normal day, humid and searing. When we landed in San Francisco, I couldn't believe how beautiful it was. I loved the zigzaggy hills and the sight of the Bay sparkling in the sunlight. But then the cold seeped through our clothes, into our bones; I felt as if I had never been warm.

I'd always wondered what America would be like, and now I knew: freezing.

A month before we moved, Mom and Dad had sat Brittany and me down for a "family conference." Dad was uncharacteristically quiet, and Mom was grave. They were both so serious I thought someone had died. "We're moving to America," Mom had said. "Dad and I have decided. Business has been bad and this is our only option. We have no more prospects here." That's all they said—the only explanation they ever gave for their decision to leave the country. But I always wondered if there was anything else—something that they weren't telling me. A month before, my parents had been planning a vacation to Disneyland Japan, and all of a sudden we were packing our bags and clearing out?

In any event, I was shocked and excited. Leaving the Philippines! But what about high school? And all my friends?

Peaches, Bing, and Con-con? What about Lola and Lolo and *Tita* Connie and *Tito* Dongdong? And all our cousins? Move? To America? Were we moving to Los Angeles? Or New York? Would we bump into Leonardo DiCaprio at the supermarket?

The rest of the month was a blur. I spent every weekend at the megamall with Peaches, and we promised each other that we would e-mail every day. Dad left for San Francisco first, so he could rent a house and start his business. He never even had a proper good-bye party. He left the country as casually as if he were leaving for a weekend at the beach. It was up to Mom to sell the house, our cars, and secure the maids' new employment with friends and families. Our chauffeur cried. He'd been with us for fifteen years—before I was even born. My grandmother stuffed twenty-five dollars into my wallet at the airport. It was more money than I ever had in my life, because according to the exchange rate, at fifty pesos to a dollar, Lola had actually given me more than twelve hundred pesos!

To prepare for our move, I had packed my collection of three hundred books into five oversized cardboard boxes. Mom and Dad promised to have them shipped to our new home. They still haven't done so. My backpack only held ten paperbacks—a couple of Harry Potter books, an *Anne of Green Gables*, and my torn copy of *Little Women*. I still mourn my lost hardbound copies of the entire Classic Treasury series (*Jungle*

Book, *David Copperfield*, *Black Beauty*). I can't afford to buy new ones. The boxes are probably sitting in my grandmother's basement somewhere, attracting dust and mold.

We didn't own any clothes suitable for cold weather, so Mom had asked her seamstress to sew matching double-breasted velvet trench coats for Brittany and me. They were stunning—a deep violet which sparkled cranberry in the light, with square pockets and yoke stitching. I wore mine the first week of school, but Whitney said I looked Amish. I never wore it again.

The plane ride was endless. On the little personal video screens they have in coach for trans-Pacific flights, I watched *Good Will Hunting* so many times that I memorized every line. (Matt Damon: "She doesn't need me. Maybe she's perfect right now." Robin Williams: "Maybe *you're* perfect right now.") I dreamed I was Minnie Driver—curly-haired and kooky but so beautiful I could wear goofy oversized sunglasses and Matt Damon would still fall in love with me.

When we arrived at the immigration counter, there were two lines: one for U.S. citizens and another for all the rest. The Americans were zipped through with barely a nod, but our line snaked down the room, past baggage claim, into the next terminal.

Mom was nervous since we were entering the country on tourist visas but were really planning to immigrate. We'd heard rumors of instant deportations, friends of friends who had been sent back to Manila the minute they set foot in San Francisco because they had overpacked, because they had answered incorrectly, because the INS officer just didn't like the way they looked. A relative who had moved to California two decades ago warned us not to pack bagoong, a salty shrimp paste that smelled like feet that Filipinos like to eat with fruit. My parents took the warnings seriously, bemoaning the fact that they would never again have bagoong for their mangos. It was only a few months later that Mom burst out laughing, out of the blue. "Who in their right mind would travel with condiments?"

But we weren't laughing when we arrived. My mother wore her tan Burberry raincoat and her Christian Dior sunglasses. She was wearing her most expensive dress, her most impressive shoes. She thought it best to disguise the fact that we were leaving our country forever, flying the coop, never going back. Who in their right mind would immigrate in designer heels? We were playing the part of rich tourists.

"Reason for visit?" the immigration officer asked, reviewing our passports (stamped, with our travels to Venice, to Singapore, to Thailand, to Luxembourg.)

"My sister is getting married," Mom lied, smiling.

"Congratulations," he said grimly. "Desired length of stay?"

"Six months. We're helping her get settled." My mother's

hands shook as she held on to her Louis Vuitton handbag.

"Taking the kids away from school?" the official asked, eyeing Brittany.

"She's only four. Not in school yet."

"And what about your other daughter?" He motioned to me.

"Oh!" Mom said, flustered. "She's—uh—she's done."

He gave me a quick once-over then stamped our passports.

Later, my mother admitted she almost peed in her shoes. She had meant that I had just graduated from elementary school, but luckily the official had mistaken her words, thinking she had meant high school, or even college. I was tall for my age, and in my velvet trench coat, I imagined I looked sophisticated and worldly. But perhaps the Homeland Security officer simply hadn't bothered to check my birth date.

I helped my mother wheel away our nine oversized suitcases, laden with all the material possessions we owned in the world. Mom had brought her Ming vases, cleverly wrapped inside Dad's trousers and filled with his socks. My sister had packed her three-story Barbie town house. There was a VCR in there somewhere, too.

We walked out to the terminal and found Dad standing past the security checkpoint. He was grinning. *"Ano?"*

"Six months!" Mom cried. "We got our six months!"

Six months was the longest time tourists were allowed to stay in the country. Dad was counting on our tourist visas lasting that long, until our immigration lawyer was able to petition his company for a business visa and eventually get us resident visas, otherwise known as green cards, so we would be able to stay in America forever.

Mom drove a ten-year-old Toyota, instead of a new Lexus. She had on her Christian Dior sunglasses, but she never wore her old shoes anymore. In Manila, she had worn only four-inch heels, delicate kidskin mules, buttery cream-colored slingbacks, or else gold leather or snakeskin or crocodile stilettos that tied around her ankles. It was a shock to see her in pink canvas sneakers from Payless for the first time. I didn't even recognize her. For one thing, I had never realized she was so short.

"Let's go shopping!" she said gaily, as she put the car in reverse and backed out of the Sears parking lot. "Want to?" she asked, peering at me in the rearview mirror.

I shrugged. "Okay."

We drove out of the mall and made our way across town, to the nearest Salvation Army store. A friend from church had advised us it was a good place to shop on a limited budget. Except for our televisions, everything we owned was second-hand. The Dalugdugans had given us a folding table and several plastic chairs for the dining room. Our brown plaid couch was from Goodwill, as were the matching chipboard bureaus in each bedroom. We couldn't afford bed frames, so we placed bricks and wooden planks under the mattresses to keep them off the floor.

When we arrived, Mom rifled through the racks as expertly and as enthusiastically as if she were still shopping at Rustan's, the high-priced department store she had favored in Manila. At Rustan's, white-gloved attendants presented her with Chanel suits and Dolce & Gabbana gowns. A man in a military uniform used a public address system to call in your car and driver when you were done shopping. ("Driver Arambullo . . . to the front, please.") We'd stand inside the frosted doors, in the air-conditioned foyer, until Mang Remus drove up with the Lexus. Three salesclerks would load up the trunk with our packages.

"Look at this! A fur coat!" Mom said, holding up a black, knee-length jacket made of fur of an indeterminate origin. The price tag was stapled to the front collar. It was one of the little details about thrift stores I found so depressing. Why did the prices have to be *stapled*? Were the clothes so unworthy of care that they couldn't even make an effort to create proper tags?

"Forty dollars." Mom sighed, patting the luxurious pelt.

"Try it on," I urged. The weather was the hardest on my mother. Like me, she was always cold. She took off her puffy 49ers jacket and hung it on a nearby hook. She struggled into the fur coat, placing it over her khaki pants and thin cotton sweater, and surveyed herself in the mirror. Her eyes shone. "It's beauti-ful," she said, turning around to see the side and back.

"What do you think?" she asked me. "Okay *ba*?"

"Get it." I nodded. I missed the days when Mom bought the same heels in three different colors.

"It's not too big?" she asked, fluffing her hair.

"No, it looks great, Mom."

It really did. Mom had a good eye for fashion. She could find vintage Oleg Cassini in a rack of polyester or unearth an Art Deco brooch in a pile of cheap goldplated trinkets. Unlike the other coats and jackets that were hanging in the fur rack, the coat Mom had picked wasn't threadbare, moth-eaten, or smelly. It had the sweep and grandeur appropriate for a 1930s movie star. You could imagine Marlene Dietrich in it.

I left my mother at the mirror to do a little shopping of my own. The store was divided into departments, just like an ordi-nary shop. On the right were men's clothes—stained T-shirts, yellowing button-downs, the occasional Charter Club three-piece wool suit. Next were the "ladies" garments, printed cotton housedresses and muumuus, acid-washed jeans, dowdy tartan skirts, a vat of acrylic sweaters, decrepit Easter bonnets, and two shelves of rotten shoes. There was even a table of underwear—but Mom and I had always tacitly agreed we would never stoop so low as to select from it.

A rack of "evening wear" contained old sixties prom dresses in garish pastel colors, and for a while there, I had a *Pretty in Pink* fantasy. Claude, playing the part of Andrew McCarthy, the rich popular boy, would ask me, the Filipino Molly Ringwald, to the Soirée, and I would sew myself a dress from an old taffeta one . . . except mine wouldn't look shapeless and weird like Molly's. I'd wear something black, with lace, and I'd fashion an asymmetrical hem that dipped low in the back but high in the front.

One thing I grudgingly admired about the Salvation Army was that everything was so very affordable. I bought two T-shirts (twenty-five cents each), one that said BENETTON in capital letters and another that still had its bedraggled Esprit label. I found an oversized black blazer and a few flannel shirts that reminded me of the one Pink wore on the cover of *Teen People*. I tried on a pair of jeans priced at three dollars. They weren't boot-leg cut, but at least they were Levi's. I even found an old cashmere sweater with only one tiny hole on the shoulder.

Dad was embarrassed that we had to shop at the Salvation Army, so Mom and I always went after work, in secret. He never set foot in it, and Mom never bought him any clothes from there. "Used clothes?" he'd say, making a face. "Yecch. Who knows who died in them?"

"It's called vintage," I would argue, defending our purchases.

It embarrassed me as well, since most of the people who shopped at the Salvation Army were either elderly or painfully indigent. Once in a while, I would notice cool-looking older kids trying on beaded cardigans or gas station attendant shirts that had "Gus" or "Johnny" on the front pockets, but they would pay for them with platinum credit cards. It was all a lark, a bit of fun, slumming, for them and it always made me angry. We were here because we couldn't afford to shop anywhere else. They had a choice. I wished they would go back to Urban Outfitters where they belonged.

"Are you ready?" Mom asked, her face flushed.

"Yes. Are you getting it?"

"I don't know—do you think I should?" she asked, clasping it tightly in her arms.

"It's really nice, Mom. Get it."

"Okay," she said. "Okay. I will!"

We walked to the cashier line, where an old man in a fedora and plaid golf pants was counting out eighty-five cents for a green cardigan. The cashier threw it into a crumpled plastic bag and handed it to him.

"Can I just hold it?" Mom asked, taking the coat away from the indifferent saleslady when it was our turn. She paid for her coat with cash from the red tin can.

I placed my choices on the table and handed over my ten dollars. Mom snatched the money out of my hand and pressed it back into my palm. "No, no—today, my treat," she said. I was only too happy to oblige.

We walked back to the Corolla. I swung my plastic bag filled with second-hand treasures while Mom cradled her new fur coat in her arms.

"Put it on," I said.

"Okay," she agreed, stuffing her football jacket in the backseat and slipping her new fur over her shoulders.

Outside the Salvation Army store, away from the racks of old, soiled, and discarded goods, it didn't look like a used coat. She put on her designer sunglasses even if it was starting to get dark outside. When she climbed into the car, she sat up a little straighter and I saw her smile at me in the rearview mirror. The setting sun shone through the auburn highlights of her hair. The dark, liquid softness of her coat matched her gold-tinted designer frames. For a moment, she looked like herself again.

FROM: queen_vee@aol.com

TO: amparo.dellarosa@info.ph.com

SENT: Sunday, October 18, 6:11 PM

SUBJECT: Shopping Spree

Hi, Peaches,

Whitney and I were so bad! We spent so much money! Mom is totally going to take away my allowance when she finds out. Here's what I bought at the mall yesterday:

- really cute flannel shirts from Abercrombie & Fitch
- T-shirts from Esprit and Benetton
- boot-cut jeans from the Gap
- black blazer and cashmere sweater from Bloomingdale's

Spending like a fiend,

V

6

Mathematical Miracles

CLAUDE CALIGARI IS my geometry partner!!

How did this happen???

Am I the luckiest girl alive???

Maybe!

It's so weird. One day, he almost runs me over with his car—a few weeks later, I have to help him graph linear equations. This is so cool.

And I owe it all to a chair.

Let me explain.

I'm in the higher math class since I'd already taken algebra in Manila so now I was in geometry with the sophomores. It's not like I'm some Asian math whiz or anything. In fact, nothing could have been further from the truth. I abhor math. I slept through fractions in second grade and I feel like I haven't caught up since.

My geometry class is a trip, though. The sophomores—led by

Stacey Bennett, Alice O'Hara, and Rebecca Wallace—went berserk a week ago Monday pretending to do yoga on their desks and totally ignoring our beleaguered geometry teacher, Miss Watkins, who completely lost it. She even threatened to beat them with her chair, which is so not cool, especially since Grosvernor is a snooty private school and Stacy's parents are on the Board of Trustees. She was fired the next day, and to make a long story short, we lost a teacher but gained a classroom full of boys.

It was too late in the semester to find a decent substitute (one who'd majored in math at Harvard and somehow couldn't get a job in Silicon Valley), so last week they decided to let us take geometry at Montclair, our "brother" school, taught by Miss Tresoro. There's been a rumor that the two schools are going to merge into one coed institution, but it's just wishful thinking. I overheard someone saying that the docents of Gros will never let it happen. Apparently, when schools go coed the girls' school always gets shafted.

Anyway, the important thing is that

CLAUDE CALIGARI IS NOW MY GEOMETRY PART-NER!

Geometry meets three times a week during A period. Grosvernor and Montclair are on this wacky college prep schedule, where classes are assigned "periods"—A, B, C, D, and so forth. And all the periods get shuffled every day, (although it's the same every week) so that sometimes geometry is the last class of the day, sometimes it's in the middle, and sometimes it's after lunch. Even lunch is on a "period" schedule, anywhere from eleven A.M. to one P.M., so that not everyone has lunch at the same time— unfortunately, I seem to have drawn the same lunch period as Whitney, Georgia, and Trish. Someone told me they plan it this way because the cafeteria is too small to have all the students in it at the same time.

Three times a week, I'm going to be sitting next to the cutest boy at Montclair. He's so popular there's even an unofficial online fan club created by an anonymous Grosvernor student devoted to chronicling his every move. We were paired up alphabetically, so it was pure luck that I got to sit next to him.

I couldn't breathe when he took the chair next to mine on Monday. I couldn't even look him in the eye. It was like being blinded by the sun. There was no way I could concentrate. All I saw was the downy blond hair on his tanned arm. I've even memorized the mole on his wrist and how the dimples creased on his left cheek. Like Tobey Maguire, he has this way of squinting which is just plain adorable.

On Wednesday afternoon he waltzed in late, blaming "practice." Apparently, he failed geometry I last semester for the second time, which explains why he's a junior in a sophomore class. He's a totally useless study partner since he understands even less than I do. And he never has his homework done.

When we sit together, I like to pretend that he's, like, my boyfriend or something—that's how close we are. It's just a matter of time before he notices me—and who knows, he might even ask for a study date, just to cover up the fact that he really wants to hang out and get to know me better. Then he'll start picking me up after school and we'll drive off in his car and everyone will be so jealous and then girls in class will start to want to talk to me and invite me to their parties or maybe even let me sit with them in the cafeteria and not get all quiet when I walk into a room, like they were just talking about me but they weren't saying anything nice.

I spent most of the class daydreaming about how romantic it would be if he suddenly discovered he was in love with me after all this time.

"Vicenza, I adore you," Claude would say. "I never noticed how well suited we are."

"Especially since we both know nothing about geometry!" I would breathe.

Then we would kiss, and the lights would go all fuzzy like they do in the movies.

Or maybe he'll simply ask me what I think of the class and how my day is and where I'm from and how come I have such an interesting name and what did I think of America. And we would embark on a twenty-first-century Pocahontas kind of romance. Riiiight.

It's going to be difficult for him to get to know me, though, because he sits with his back to me—to chat and trade notes with Rebecca and Stacey. The three of them gossiped about Lake Tahoe ski trips and black diamond lanes and which mountain rocks and how badly "Becks" took a spill last time.

"Claude!" Miss Tresoro called.

He paid no attention. "Omigod, you were, like, a cyclone down that hill!" He laughed, whooping loudly.

"Shhh! You're so mean to me!" Rebecca pouted.

"He's right, though—you were like a snowball. It was so funny!" Stacey added, leaning in so that her long russet-colored hair brushed Claude's shoulder.

"Claude!" the geometry teacher warned again.

He cocked an eyebrow. "Yeah?"

"Would you like to share what you're discussing with Rebecca with the rest of the class?"

"Sure!" he said with a huge, goofy grin. "I was just telling Becks that she really should get a Burton board this year. Especially if she's going to kick my ass when we get to Timberline, which is highly unlikely."

Miss Tresoro frowned but you could tell she didn't really mean it. Claude had that effect on everyone. He zigzagged and tap-danced lightly through life. It was just too bad he couldn't schmooze his way to an A.

"I really think she should think about a Lib Tech Dark instead," Miss Tresoro replied. "It's all about freestylin', right, Rebecca?" It was all snowbabble as far as I was concerned. But Miss Tresoro was hip. She was down. She wore low-waisted slacks and leather jackets. She was a Gros alumna and she knew her way around. She could let Claude walk in late, let Alice and Stacey whisper between lessons all they wanted, but unlike our old geometry teacher, the class respected and admired her. She would never walk into a classroom with the lights off only to find her students sitting Indian-style on their desks, meditating.

"Good call!" Claude agreed.

"All right, can we please get back to isosceles triangles now?" She turned to the blackboard and class resumed uninterrupted for the next half hour. As the final bell rang, Miss Tresoro handed out the results of Monday's exam.

I frowned when I saw I had gotten 72 out of 100. I couldn't afford a C minus in geometry if I wanted to keep my scholarship.

"Damn," Claude said when he saw his test result. "Do you know this stuff?"

"Me?" I squeaked.

He had never paid any attention to me before. He had said

exactly two words to me since our classes had been merged: "Move over." It seemed I was taking too much room on our shared study table.

"Um, not really," I said, showing him my paper.

"That's a lot better than what I got," he said, crunching his test into a ball and morosely chucking it into the trash. "If I don't pass geometry this semester, I'll get kicked off the lacrosse team. I'm already on academic probation."

I nodded in sympathy. But I didn't really know what to do, since I was barely passing the subject myself. But I wanted to help—he looked so glum.

"That's too bad," I ventured.

"You said it," he said. "I'm screwed."

He picked up his backpack and we started walking out of class together—TOGETHER—as if we do this all the time. As if this is a normal occurrence in my life, that boys, like, *talk* to me. As if we were, like, friends or something.

Geometry is my last class of the day on Wednesdays, and suddenly I had an irresistible, irrational impulse to ask him out or something—*want to go get a smoothie on Union Street?* I could just imagine it, the two of us, sipping from the same biggie cup. He was still chatting about his geometry problems, when I opened my mouth. "Claude?"

But I realized he had already gone. He was running up the

block to walk with Rebecca and Stacey.

"Hey, Becks, wait up," I heard him call to them. "We bowling tonight? Wanna come out with Tuna and the guys?" He made plans to meet them at Rock and Bowl, the bowling alley in the Haight.

I blushed a lot, and hoped to God he hadn't heard me call his name. And I felt a little depressed about being left behind, and it was then I understood that it wasn't ever going to happen with me and Claude. I was just living in my head, like I always do. Claude would never in a million years ever think of inviting me to go anywhere. He's a popular boy; I'm nobody. He has an online fan club. (With five-dollar membership dues—I had to use my mom's Visa and tell her it was for a school project. True enough!) People barely remember who I am.

I followed them out of the main doors, feeling completely alone, when I noticed Isobel waiting for me outside.

So she's not the cutest guy at Montclair Academy, but at least she's someone who knows I'm alive.

Isobel wanted to know everything about taking a class over at the boys' school. There really wasn't a lot to tell. I explained that I never saw anyone other than the guys who were in our class, and with the exception of Claude they were all unexceptional (read: not cute), to her great disappointment.

"How's that boy?" Isobel asked. She called Claude "that boy

who broke my mirror" but had recently shortened it to simply "that boy."

"Flunking."

"Is an idiot?"

"Isobel, just because he isn't good in math doesn't mean he's stupid," I protested, feeling a little insulted. Isobel was in advanced trigonometry. She was in the accelerated honors math/science program. Her father was a member of the Engineering Department at Stanford.

"Geometry is *trop facile*. It's just logic and theorem."

She handed me a DVD she'd burned on her iMac of an underground cult alternate ending of the first Spider-Man movie some Internet freak spliced together that was only available online. "This one is buggin'. Tobey's got his shirt off in all the added scenes!"

"Awesome!" I said, grateful for the present.

"Come shopping on Polk Street?" she asked, hopping on her Vespa. "There's new stuff at Trash and Vaudeville."

"Can't," I said. "I have to help my mom at the cafeteria." School let out at three, and just that morning my parents broke the news that from now on I was expected to help cover the six o'clock dinner rush. We had started to close a little later on weeknights to take advantage of the mall food court closing at five.

"*Tant pis*. Next time." She kissed me on both cheeks, something I was still getting used to, and drove off down the hill, waving. *"A bientôt, chérie!"*

"Au revoir!" I chéried back, blowing multiple kisses to the wind.

"Those two are such freaks," I heard Georgia say behind my back. I refused to turn around, because I didn't want her to know I had heard, and I didn't want to hear Whitney agree with her. I was too embarrassed because I believed they were right.

Heads up people! Sighted at Rock and Bowl on Wednesday night, C.C. himself with a big group. Was that Stacey Bennett with another hickey? Did Tuna and Trish hook up over malted milk shakes? Who cares? Is this site called welovetuna.com? Nooo. We hear C.C. scored a big 240! Not just a great lacrosse forward but the guy to beat on the lanes, too! Our sources tell us he has a new girlfriend, as yet undisclosed. Maybe it's one of the Gros girls in his geometry class? Has Monty gone coed? Hell, no! But a few lucky gals are being shipped over for math class. Talk about higher education! So keep your eyes peeled, chiquitas! And check out the latest pics from the Montclair vs. Warrington game! Hubba-hubba, hottie!

7

The Reality of Another Weekend at Home

O N THE RIGHT-HAND TV screen, a blond, overweight woman in a tight-fitting bustier was arguing with her interior designer, a hyperkinetic gay man who was insisting she allow him to sew silk-screened portraits of her on her couch pillows; on the center screen, former celebrities were bickering over who had eaten the last of the yogurt in the fridge; and on the left screen, a real-estate mogul with a really bad comb-over was chewing out a group of sullen aspiring MBAs.

Our living room was home to three television monitors and VCRs—the better to tape reality shows with. As part of Dad's import-export business, he exported VCR tapes of the latest American reality shows to Filipino video stores. Filipinos can't get enough of the reality craze, and since local stations were so behind they were broadcasting only the second season of *Survivor* there was a thriving black market for newer, smuggled

American reality-television shows. I know, because I used to be a rabid consumer of the same. The video store at the megamall would always call the minute the latest episode of *The Bachelor* or *American Idol* arrived from the airport.

I never thought that I would be on the other end of the supply chain. My cousin Norbert owned one of the biggest video store chains in Manila, and Dad knew a friend who knew a friend who was a pilot on Philippine Airlines. Captain Punsalang could easily smuggle the tapes into the country, and a thriving cottage industry was born in our living room. I was the best taper in the family, meaning I could watch three different shows at once and expertly pause the VCRs when the commercials came on to create a seamless product. In fact, I was too good. We got a request from Norbert saying that his customers actually wanted us to keep the commercials in. It turned out people were just as fascinated by the latest advertising campaigns as by the shows themselves. Filipinos had just discovered rotisserie barbecues.

One thing about Filipinos—we love trends. When the ballroom-dancing craze swept the nation, everyone from eighty-year-old grandmothers to second-graders learned how to fox-trot, cha-cha, and tango. My friend Con-con's mother left her dad for her twenty-two-year-old ballroom dancing teacher. When pashminas were in vogue, we swathed ourselves in those woolly wraps in every color—regardless of the outside temperature. You would walk around the city on a typically hot and humid day, and you'd see all the women from Forbes Park and Dasmariñas wearing pashminas and fanning themselves silly.

I taped reality shows almost every night. From the *Real World* to *Fear Factor*, I watched them all. I had my favorites—the new show where twenty grossly overweight people tried to lose weight and were kicked out if they were caught eating chocolate cake was a stunner, and the one where international mail-order brides competed for old geezers with wrinkles and liver spots was another (my money was on the Russian to go all the way and win the big prize: marriage and citizenship to a seventy-year-old who owned an aboveground pool company).

Mom and Dad had no stomach for these shows. They liked "quality" programming, like *60 Minutes*, *20/20*, and *Primetime Live*. Anything hosted by Diane Sawyer was fine by them—even if it was sensationalist dreck like yet another special on Princess Di ("Diana's Secret Heartache Finally Revealed!").

The other month when Diane Sawyer reported on the rash of "identity thefts," Dad was convinced he was a victim of the crime when Blockbuster video called to ask him about a tape he had returned. The store had called because Mr. Arambullo had returned a tape containing sitcoms rather than *Bruce Almighty*. "Identity theft! Identity theft!" Dad had yelled. "I never borrowed *Bruce Almighty*! Someone's using my card!"

"They must be some pretty honest thieves, Dad," I pointed out, "since they actually tried to *return* the movie. And paid for it." Still, Dad couldn't be talked out of it. He even nailed our mailbox shut in accordance with Diane Sawyer's advice. So now we had to pick up our mail from underneath our doormat.

Brittany was too young to work the VCR controls, so it was left up to me to make sure we had enough reel in the tapes, that they were labeled correctly, and then packed up in the brown cardboard boxes for Captain Punsalang to take on his next trip home.

The real-estate mogul fired the toothy blond stripper turned "marketing manager." Damn! There went five bucks to Isobel.

"*Tama na*, time for dinner," Dad said, patting my shoulder. I waited until the closing credits rolled and joined my family at the table.

We rarely ate in restaurants anymore. McDonald's was a treat reserved for Sundays after church. Our greatest ambition in life was to eat at Outback Steakhouse. On the very, very rare occasions we did go out to eat in a real restaurant (on birthdays, holidays, or their anniversary) to Sizzler, Chili's, or Applebee's, Mom would pick at her food, turn up her nose, and say, "Ugh. I can make this better at home," almost as if she were insulted.

She was usually right, but I was so happy to be filling my plate with thirty shrimp from Red Lobster that I didn't care. Sometimes I would even argue with her. "No, you can't! You put *sugar* in the spaghetti, Mom! They don't do that at the Olive Garden!"

Dad was setting the table, so I helped him lay out the place mats, napkins, silverware, plates, salad bowls, and water glasses. Mom brought out a garlicky-smelling vegetable pinakbet full of okra and bitter melon; a platter of dark, smoky strips of beef tapa, fluffy white rice, a very salty fish sauce called patis; and the precious bagoong, which we were happy to find at an Asian market. Dinner was by far the highlight of each day, even if it was far from how it used to be. In Manila, we had a majestic round table in the formal dining room that could seat twelve people. Uniformed maids stood behind our chairs and fanned us with banana leaves. In the middle of our table here was a lazy Susan Mom had bought in Chinatown. I liked to spin it past Brittany and pretend she would never get anything to eat, just to make her cry.

"How was school today?" Mom asked, as she layered my plate with vegetables, meat, and rice.

"Okay," I mumbled. "I got an A on my English essay."

Whenever my parents asked about school, I told them about my teachers. The sad thing about my life was that I've realized the only reason school is in any way tolerable is because of my teachers. Unlike my classmates, who avoid me—except for Isobel, who isn't too popular herself—all the teachers like me. But then, what's not to like? I'm practically the cliché of the perfect student—quiet, diligent, respectful. They all marvel over my "beautiful" handwriting. In Manila, each convent school teaches its students a signature style of calligraphy. "This is a work of art," Mrs. Malloney, our art history teacher said, when I first handed in a written test. I was proud of it until I saw Whitney's blotted notebook. Everything was written in scrawled chicken-scratch-like block letters, like a five-year-old's.

"Another A? That's great. Congratulations!" Mom said, beaming at me.

"Um, Mom? Do you think I could get that new jacket we saw at the mall the other day?" I asked, pleading silently with my eyes, even though I knew the answer already. But the weather was starting to get really cold, and I was desperate to lose the 49ers jacket.

"What jacket?" Dad asked.

"It's nothing." I shrugged. "Just a black jacket." A plain black wool jacket that would render me invisible, that is, one that would make me look like everyone else at school, at least on the outside. I was so tired of wearing the puffy football jacket inside out.

"What's wrong with that violet trench coat we had made?" Mom asked. "You never wear it anymore."

"How much is this new coat?" Dad said.

I hated this part. "Not too bad. Not more than a hundred dollars. It's, like, seventy-five."

Dad looked down at his plate. Mom said nothing.

"Please? Please?"

"*Iha*, you know we would love to be able to say yes, but there's just no money for things like that anymore." Mom sighed.

"Maybe next year?" Dad asked, smiling hopefully.

"Okay," I mumbled. I shouldn't even have tried. "I never get anything anymore," I muttered to myself.

Brittany shot me a sympathetic look from across the table. She was only five years old, but she already knew the deal.

After the air cleared a little from the heaviness of my disappointment, Mom and Dad talked about how the cafeteria was doing. Mom told us about how the old biddies in Housewares had begun to order the more expensive daily specials instead of their usual tuna salad half sandwiches, and Dad regaled us with funny stories about the Indian guys next door to his office who owned a limousine business and chauffeured visiting celebrities around town, like the Rock, Carmen Electra, and Carrot Top.

Mom and Dad both worried about our other relatives who were also immigrating. One of my uncles, a cardiologist in Manila, was planning to scheme for an American green card by posing as a migrant farmworker, since a recent U.S. government act had granted field-workers full asylum. Another cousin had a Canadian resident visa but lived and worked illegally in Detroit as a mechanic since his job wasn't part of NAFTA.

Hearing them talk like this, it always seemed to me that everyone in Manila was desperate to leave. Some of our relatives were even moving to Australia, since it had an easier immigration process than the States. Canada was also a popular destination because once you were approved, you were eligible for citizenship in three short years. But my parents were optimists, dreamers, idealists. They wanted the big one—the jackpot: America. They didn't want to settle for anything less. My cousins in Toronto swore up and down that their adopted land was tops. "We have digital cable, Starbucks, and the original Club Monaco. Michael J. Fox, Peter Jennings, and Mike Myers are all Canadian. Canada— it's *just as good!*" But we didn't believe them.

At the end of the meal, while Mom served fried bananas with sugar and poured coffee, Dad opened up discussion on his favorite topic. Also known as "WHAT THE ARAMBULLO FAMILY WOULD DO IF WE EVER WON THE LOTTERY." Dad loved to fantasize about what our life would be like if we ever hit lotto (he pronounced it "ladda" in an attempt at an American accent). He continued to buy a lottery ticket every day and never failed to check the numbers in the newspapers in the mornings. If the jackpot was over fifty million dollars, he upped his ante to five.

"I think I'll buy a car. A Denali. What do you think, Mom? Or should we get a Lexus again? Or maybe a Beamer this time?"

He sipped his coffee and a faraway look of happiness settled in his eyes. "What about you, girls? What would you do, Brit?"

"I would go to Disneyland every day!" Brittany chirped. It was her dream to visit the furry-costumed oversize mice and the shellacked princesses. Every Halloween since she was two years old, my little sister has dressed up as a Disney movie princess, from Cinderella to Belle to Mulan. Nothing made her happier than wearing a tiara. I predicted nothing but heartache in her teenage years.

Whenever my family had this conversation, I always volunteered the same intense, feverish wish. If we ever won the lottery, *I would drop out of school.* If we ever won the lottery, *I would never go back to Grosvernor ever again.* I could do whatever I wanted. We would be millionaires, so I wouldn't even need an education.

Mom never participated in these discussions. She didn't approve. I had a feeling she thought they were silly.

"What would you do, Mom?" Brittany and I asked, badgering her like we always did to tell us her heart's desire. "Tell us what you would do if we won lotto!"

"Ah, who knows? Why think of it? We'll never win."

"Don't say that!" the three of us chorused, scandalized. Dad looked hurt. It was pure blasphemy. Brittany and I always believed everything our father told us. He would make it come true, he would. Dad would find a way. Someday we'd be rich again, and live happily ever after. Dad would buy his Lexus, Brittany would ride It's a Small World till she puked, I would be excused from having to attend high school, and Mom—Mom would get to do whatever it was she never told us she wanted to do.

The next evening I was still dreaming of my new life as an Olsen twin as I popped in the tapes for the night's batch of reality TV programming. How jealous everyone would be of my new Miss Sixty jeans, Tommy Hilfiger tops, and Puma sneakers. Claude would finally ask me out. I would get a cuter handbag than Trish's. And I'd drive a Mini when I was sixteen, a jaunty red one, like the one Alexandra Arleghetti, the president of the junior class, drove.

"V, phone for you," Mom called from the kitchen, where she was chopping pork back for the longanisas. To make a little more money on the side, Mom sold her homemade pork sausages to the few Filipino friends she had made at church. Her longanisas were in great demand. They were salty and sweet, and the perfect accompaniment to a "healthy" Filipino breakfast. Heart attack on a plate, Dad called it.

"For me?" I asked. It must be a mistake. Nobody ever called

me at home. Peaches did once, and we talked long-distance for hours. But it was so expensive that she was grounded for two months afterward. I never even used my cell phone. What was the point? No one ever needed to speak to me so bad. The only people who called me on it were my parents, to find out what time I was getting to the cafeteria from school.

I quickly checked the TVs and ran to the kitchen. Mom sat in front of a large, frozen slab of pork fat, kneading and warming it up so she could chop it into small pieces. It was hard work, and her hands alternately froze from the cold or turned red from the effort of running a knife through the thick skin. The pork fat felt like dry ice to the touch—so cold it burned. It caused blisters and frostbite. After chopping, she added it into a huge plastic basin of ground meat. It was so punishingly hard to mix that only Dad was strong enough to do it. Mom and I took turns mixing at first, but we didn't have the strength. Afterward, Mom pushed the combination into a meat grinder and stuffed it into sausage casings. Dad had done a day's worth of market research by visiting all the Filipino supermarkets to come up with the right price: $5 a tray. Which worked out to a profit of about fifty-five cents for each package.

I gave Mom a quick squeeze on her shoulder and picked up the phone dangling from the hook. "Hello?"

"*Bonsoir!*" rang the cheery voice of Isobel.

"Hey, what's up?" I said, trying to sound casual as I ran back to the living room with the extralong cord. Isobel and I always hung out at school, but she spent every weekend with her French friends sneaking out to swanky North Beach bars and martini lounges because they all had fake IDs. Veronique Delay and Leslie Foucault, who Isobel knew in Paris, were enrolled at the Lycée Français. Isobel didn't go there because her parents thought the French school was too insular, plus, it didn't have as extensive a math program as Gros.

"*Rien.* Leslie and Veronique didn't want to go clubbing," she explained.

"Too bad," I sympathized. But I was happy to merit her attention on a Saturday night for once.

"I'm ennui. What are you doing?"

"Taping reality shows." I explained about Dad's business. I wasn't shy about telling Isobel the truth about my life. She told me her family lived in ritzy St. Francis Woods, but she said their house was the smallest one there and filled with old, dusty, over-stuffed furniture.

"Are you taping *Trading Spaces*?" she asked. Isobel once told me she thought reality shows were bunk and, quoting her dad, "the death of the culture Americaine" but even she was addicted to home-makeover programs.

"Yeah, isn't it awful? Those raffia headboards have got to go."

"Yuck, what is that color are they putting on the walls? Fuchsia?"

"Check out the seashell headboard!"

"Ooh, *Wonder Boys* on HBO!"

I flipped to it during a commercial. We swooned over Tobey's white ribbed tank top. Isobel wanted to get "Mrs. Maguire" inked above her derriere, but I talked her out of it for now.

"There's a bonfire at Baker Beach tonight," Isobel mentioned casually.

"I know," I said. (Claude's fan site had even provided a map to the exact location.)

"Is that boy going?"

"Most likely."

"You know, he and Whitney are bangin'," Isobel said. She had just watched *8 Mile* and had started to insert hip-hop phrases into her speech.

"No way! I thought she had a boyfriend in Carmel." (Jeez, you really couldn't believe everything you read. The site reported Claude was "happily single.")

"They broke up. I heard Georgia talking about it in English," Isobel said.

"So he's really dating her?"

"*J'écoute* he's taking her to the Soirée." A small knot formed in my stomach. So it was true. He really was dating Whitney. He was taken. I mourned our five-second conversation in geometry. And I thought we had really connected!

"Are you going?" I asked.

"Me? No! I told you. It's moronic. What about *vous*?"

"Me neither."

"Should we make a pact that we both won't go to the stupid Soirée?" she asked.

"Okay. I promise."

"Moi aussi."

We were on the phone for the next two hours, watching as different sets of neighbors discovered what atrocities or wonderments their friends had inflicted on their homes, until I finally fell asleep on the phone to the sound of agitated complaints and ecstatic commotion.

FROM: queen_vee@aol.com
TO: amparo.dellarosa@info.ph.com
SENT: Sunday, October 25, 8:01 PM
SUBJECT: sat night fever

Hi, Peaches—

Your sister's debut sounded so fun! I wish I was there. I can't believe your parents wouldn't allow you to bring a date though! Was Rufi mad?

Last night, Whit, Georgia, Trish, and I met the guys at Baker Beach for a bonfire. We roasted marshmallows and hot dogs, and Claude brought his guitar. I wore my new Esprit T-shirt, but I should have brought my sweater because it was so *malamig*. The fog suddenly rolled in, and I finally discovered what "goose bumps" are.

Whitney and Claude sat next to each other. Do you think that means anything? I think she might like him, too! What am I going to do? Wouldn't that suck?

Love,

V

8

Clown-skull Book Covers Rule

THE WORST THING about working at the cafeteria after school is the utter lack of sunlight, windows, and any semblance of fresh air. We're located all the way in the back of the store, and the fluorescent lights make everything look green.

I hated doing my homework there. The table behind the counter was rickety, and I always had to lay out all my papers unevenly. It was Monday afternoon, and I was totally pitying myself for being stuck inside doing homework when I could be watching Claude at the lacrosse game. So far, I'd only been able to catch one match, thanks to the Spirit bus and Mom giving me the odd afternoon off from the cafeteria.

Half the semester was over, and I still didn't know a rhombus from a trapezoid. Claude was no help either. He didn't even show up to class half the time. We had a midterm coming up in geometry and we were both hopeless.

Annoyed at a particularly irritating question (How DOES one

prove two triangles are congruent? More important, who really cares?), I picked up *The Fountainhead* instead. I decided it was my Most Favorite Book of All Time. If they ever remade the movie, I thought Tobey would make an excellent Howard Roark, the suffering architect (who was described as a redhead, but that was a minor point—Tobey could dye his hair, just like he did for *Seabiscuit*). I had just gotten to the moment when Dominique, the feisty heiress, declared her love for Howard, when Paul the stock boy walked in, wearing his trademark red baseball cap.

He came in every afternoon on his break, and I'd gotten used to seeing him around after four o'clock. He usually asked for a Pepsi (sometimes a Kit Kat, too), sat down at a back table, and left after fifteen minutes. He always said "Hey" when he entered and "See ya" when he walked out. The cafeteria was usually deserted when he was there, making us the only two people in it, since most of the employees liked to take their afternoon breaks in the mall, not that I could blame them.

"Hey . . . Vi-*sen*-za." He smiled, pulling out his headphones on his MP3 player, which was blasting so loudly, I had heard it from across the room.

"It's Vi-*chen*-za, but most people just call me V," I said in a rush. It's weird. I don't even think he's cute. But I just get all jittery around boys, no matter who they are. It's not like I like him—I mean, first of all, he's got those braces, and he's always wearing an ugly Papa Roach or Rancid T-shirt under his ratty Sears uniform shirt.

"Are you at Mills?" he asked, naming a public school in our area.

"No, I go to school in the city. Grosvernor. It's a private school," I said, somewhat embarrassed and hoping he wouldn't think I was some kind of snob. I had begged my parents to let me attend the local public school. I craved the anonymity I imagined a big school would bring. It was somewhat difficult to disappear in a class of thirty perfect girls.

He shook his head. "I guess that explains the uniform. I should have known."

I suddenly wished I had changed out of my ugly gray skirt and cranberry blazer.

"Frosh?"

"Um-hm."

"I'm a sophomore at Hillside."

Why is he telling me this? I wondered. Not that I didn't already know that about him. As far as I could tell, half the junior salesclerks in Cosmetics had crushes on him. Laurie, this loudmouth who worked in Housewares talked about him all the time. Once I realized it was Paul she was talking about, my ears pricked up whenever they chatted about him. She and her crew were always mooning over him during break, talking about how his muscles bulged when he picked up the washer-dryers or how cute his butt looked in his 501's. I already knew he was a sophomore, lived in San Mateo, and liked to surf.

"Wanna listen to something cool?" he asked.

"Sure." I shrugged.

He handed me his headphones and I stuck them in my ears gingerly. He turned down the volume a bit, and I heard jangly guitars playing and a low voice growling a surprisingly plaintive, catchy tune.

"It's good. Who is it?" I asked.

"You really think it's good?" He smiled, cocking an eyebrow.

"Yeah." I nodded, getting into it. It had a hard edge, but the lyrics were kind of nice. It was some sort of love song.

"It's me," he said, "and a couple of guys. We're kind of in a band."

"No way!" I reached over and turned it up a little more. It was definitely his voice—deep and kind of gravelly. Funny that I didn't notice before. "Did you write it?"

"No, Led Zeppelin did." He laughed. "But I'm getting some of my own stuff together," he explained, as I handed him back his earphones. I suddenly felt shy and a little self-conscious about the intimacy of having something in my ears that was just in his.

"Well, it's really good. You guys ever play anywhere?"

"Nah," he said. "It's just a hobby. It's not like I really think

I'm going to be some guitar god or anything. I'm not that much in denial. Besides, the corporate-industrial-music complex has totally ruined the world."

"What, like MTV and stuff?" Jeez, I loved MTV. What was his deal? I didn't peg him to be such a cynic.

"Yeah, MTV, radio—it's all corporate rock. There's nothing real out there anymore."

"That's not true," I argued. "And, besides, it's just entertainment. You shouldn't take it so seriously."

"No, music matters, man." He shook his head. "That's the worst thing about the world right now—everything is trivialized into entertainment. What about passion? Art? Soul?"

"You're telling me Britney Spears doesn't have a soul?" I joked.

He made a face. "How can you listen to that crap?"

"I like Britney," I defended. "Give the girl a break. She's been through some tough times."

"V, you disappoint me," he said, shaking his head and looking down at the counter. "Oh man! And don't tell me you're reading *that*!" he said, flicking his thumb at my copy of *The Fountainhead*.

"What do you mean?" I asked, annoyed. Ayn Rand was a genius! She was a philosopher! What would some Sears stock boy know?

"That's a *terrible* book!" he said. "She started a cult. She was a dangerous person. That book is incredibly dogmatic and manipulative. It's not a novel. It's a . . . whatchamacallit . . . a manifesto . . . a rant!"

"Have you ever read it?" I asked.

"Yes and believe me, it's even worse than listening to teen pop. At least Britney doesn't try to tell you how to think."

Only how to dress, but I didn't want to seem like I was coming around to his way of thinking, so I just shrugged.

"You don't believe me, do you?" he teased.

"No, no . . ." I said, not wanting to be rude.

"Look her up sometime. You'll see what I mean."

"All right," I said coolly, even if I had no intention of doing so.

I gave him his Pepsi and his Kit Kat before he even asked for them.

"Thanks," he said, and handed me exact change. I put it away in the cash register and went back to my reading, still a little annoyed by his criticism.

I peeked over the pages and watched him sit down at the nearest table. He pulled out a worn paperback and began to read.

Even if we didn't see eye to eye on pop culture, I still liked having him there. It felt oddly comfortable, like, even if we were alone, we were being alone together.

After fifteen minutes, he stood up and walked over to the counter. What now? I wondered.

He stared askance at my book, as if the mere sight of it caused him pain. "I really hate seeing someone waste her time on it. You deserve to read something more rewarding."

"Yeah, like what?"

"Like this." He smiled, pulling out a battered copy of Stephen King's *It* from his back pocket and laying it on the tiled counter next to the cash register. I scrutinized both books side by side—the Stephen King with its silly clown-skull cover and the Ayn Rand, with its cool Art Deco graphics. Stephen King? Give me a break! I waved off the book, inadvertently brushing the back of his hand.

"You've never read any Stephen King?"

"No." I shuddered. I hated horror books. And Stephen King was a pulp fiction writer—cheap trash as far as I was concerned. I prided myself on being a little high-minded when it came to literature—I'd already read the first volume of Proust's *Remembrance of Things Past*—not that I could understand any of it—and had just devoured Kafka's *The Trial* for Honors English. Dr. Avilla said I was reading at college level. I discovered Ayn Rand all by myself in the library. I didn't have time for Stephen King.

"Take it," he said, pushing it toward me.

"I don't really—"

"No, seriously—you should read it, it's a great book."

"Okay," I said reluctantly. Whatever.

Paul looked at his watch. His wrist, I noticed, was so knobby it stuck straight out of his arm. His arms were long, tanned, and freckled. "I've gotta go. Break's over." He downed the last of his Pepsi. "Can I?" he asked, motioning to the trash can behind me.

"Sure," I said, moving out of the way.

He pretended to dribble and shot it in an arc. It bounced off the top and rolled down the floor.

"Oops!"

"I'll get it," I said, but he was already behind the counter and bending over to reach for it. "Sorry about that," he said as he straightened up. He was so tall I only came up to the bottom of his chin. I'd never noticed that before—it's kind of hard to gauge from behind the cash register.

"You gonna read that book?"

"Maybe," I said, running a finger on the well-worn spine.

"All right. See ya."

"See ya."

He walked out of the cafeteria, swinging the doors behind him. I put down *The Fountainhead* and stared at the ugly clown head laughing at me from the cover of the grotty Stephen King book. I opened to the first page, where he had scribbled his name, Paul Hartwell in the top right-hand corner.

I opened the cover of *The Fountainhead* where I had written my name, Vicenza Arambullo, in the top right-hand corner as well.

FROM: queen_vee@aol.com
TO: amparo.dellarosa@info.ph.com
SENT: Tuesday, November 3, 7:30 PM
SUBJECT: present!

Dear Peaches,

DYING!!! Claude was so sweet yesterday. I went over to his house in the afternoon to watch his band practice. Yes, he's in a band! Isn't he so talented? He plays lead guitar. He writes all the songs. Maybe he'll even dedicate one to me, like Chris Martin did to Gwyneth! When I left, he handed me a present! A book I've been dying to read. He even wrote the sweetest dedication in the front. Do you think this means he likes me?

Still confused,

V

9

The Last American Virgin?

I'VE BEEN IN this country for almost four months now, and I really don't think I'm that strange. Sure, my parents are a little weird and I just moved here and everything, but most of the time I feel just as American as anyone else. I bought a Clay Aiken album (for my mom, but I secretly listen to it all the time). I wear Gap jeans. I have a favorite Pizza Hut pizza. But yesterday I found out how truly, totally out of it I am. It happened in gym class. Whitney was going up to everybody to ask them questions for this "survey" she was taking.

Lately, she has all these projects she's working on all the time. If it's not about getting a theme for the Soirée (they decided to base it on *Titanic* although I don't know how they'll manage to turn the hotel ballroom into a sinking ship), it's getting everyone to sign petitions to convince the school to provide Zone meals in the cafeteria.

I thought it was just another of her dumb pet causes. She

really thinks she's something else. The other day she lectured the class about the dangers of expired mascara, even if she hardly wears any makeup. She got all dramatic, too, telling us how she came so close to dying when her Lancôme went bad. Isobel and I just rolled our eyes.

During gym, Whitney went up to each girl in the line, as we waited our turn on the tennis court. She had a stack of typewritten pages with her, which girls were filling out, using each other's backs to write on. Everyone was giggling and blushing.

When she got to me, she looked skeptical. "Ever hit home base?" she asked, a pen poised over her notebook.

"Excuse me?" I asked. "What's this all about?"

"Sex. You know. Wait—don't tell me. Are you, like, a *virgin*?"

I was so shocked I dropped my tennis racket.

"So, are you?" she asked, sizing me up.

"Uh, yeah." I nodded. I'm fourteen years old. Wasn't everyone?

"Thought so," she said, smirking as she marked a check in an empty column. I peeked over and saw tons of checks in the "Dirty Thirds" column, and wondered what it meant.

"You won't be needing this then," she said, snickering, as she passed a sheet of paper over to Georgia.

I heard them whispering and pointing at me, hissing the

word "virgin" as if it was some kind of insult.

What's so wrong with being a virgin at fourteen? I didn't even know it was possible to have sex that early. Was I that naïve?

That afternoon, when I got to the Sears cafeteria, I called Isobel on my cell. Hers was the only number programmed in it. I had to ask her a geometry question anyway. I'd taken to calling her whenever I got stuck. She was like a human mathematical database with a funny accent. She answered her phone after a few rings.

"*Comment?*"

"Hi, it's me."

"*Allo!* You're missing the biggest sale at Rolo's!"

"Like I have the money anyway."

"Don't worry. If I see anything you might like, I buy it for you." Isobel was like that. Unfortunately, I wasn't a big fan of gold lamé.

"Hey, Iz. What's a dirty third?" I asked, momentarily forgetting my geometry problem.

"*Comment?*"

"Did you get that poll Whitney was taking today?" I asked.

"Oh, *le sex poll?*"

"Yeah."

"What about it?" she asked.

"Did you get a copy?"

"Uh-huh. And Georgia e-mailed everyone a copy, too."

I felt a stab of hurt that I hadn't even merited the online version. "Can you send it to me?" I asked Isobel.

"Sure."

Isobel filled me in on all the bases. "No big deal," she said. "I don't even think half these girls have done it. If they say they have, they are deranging."

"Deranging?"

"Um, not to tell the truth?"

"Lying."

"*Oui.*"

"Have you?"

"Of course." She sniffed. "Twice. With my boyfriend, Sam, in New York." Right. Isobel's eighteen-year-old boyfriend who was a nightclub DJ and a freshman at NYU.

"Is not a big deal," she assured.

"Do you think Whitney's done it?"

"Who knows? Is so dumb. Did you see the questionnaire she was handing out? Which is a guy's most erogenous zone? What kind of condom you prefer? I threw it away."

I was aghast. I didn't mention that I planned to remain a virgin until I got married. Just like every good Filipino girl is supposed to—except for one of my cousins, who got knocked up when she was fifteen, but we're not supposed to talk about that. I didn't see anything wrong with waiting. I was having a hard time imagining French-kissing a guy, let alone doing . . . well . . . that.

Claude would understand. Like a gentleman, he would wait until we had graduated from college and had a proper church wedding with seventeen bridesmaids (I have a lot of cousins). I practiced writing his name next to mine on all my notebooks. Mrs. Vicenza Caligari. Mrs. Claude Caligari. Mrs. Vicenza Arambullo-Caligari.

If I couldn't have Tobey Maguire, I would settle for Claude. If Claude were my boyfriend, I would become the most popular girl at Gros (even more popular than Whitney, because unlike her, I would use my powers for Good rather than Evil).

"Americans are so puritanical," Isobel firmly declared. "Why take a poll to find out how to make out? Did she need tips? Just pick up *Cosmo*. The whole thing was so ridiculous. Anyway, I need to try something on. Telephone you later?"

"Oh wait, I totally forgot to ask you. How do I measure two acute angles? It's the last question on my homework and I can't get it."

"*Pardon?* Read the whole thing to me."

"In a right triangle, one of the acute angles is two times as large as the other acute angle. Find the measure of the two acute angles."

"That's it?"

"Yep."

"*Vous* cannot do this on your own?"

"Are you going to help me or not?"

Isobel harrumphed, like she always did when she thought I was being slow. "It's so easy, chérie! In a right triangle, the right angle is always ninety degrees. And the sum of all angles is one hundred eighty degrees which means—"

"I don't need the theory. Just the answer."

"You'll never learn." She sighed.

"Just give it to me, please?"

"Sixty degrees."

"Goddess! Thanks!"

"Cheater," she said. "You're welcome. *Mais*, I've really got to go now. I want to try on this Lycra catsuit."

I shuddered to think what leopard-print atrocity she was going to purchase now, said good-bye, and scribbled down the answer before I forgot it.

FROM: queen_vee@aol.com

TO: amparo.dellarosa@info.ph.com

SENT: Thursday, November 5, 7:30 PM

SUBJECT: bases loaded!

Dear Peaches,

    It was a school night, but Mom let me go over to
Georgia's with Whitney and Trish for a sleepover last night
and we had a looong discussion about really important stuff.
We even put together this fun poll. (See attached!) You were
right about second base. I'm attaching a breakdown of how
it goes. They all said they'd hooked up tons of times, so I
said I did, too. Even though YOU know I would NEVER
(well, maybe first base).

Later,

V

DOCUMENT ATTACHED: LOVEPOLL.DOC

10

Catwalking Down the Aisle

E WERE LATE for church today and it was all my fault.

Actually it's Mom's fault.

Every Sunday Mom wakes us up at an ungodly hour to get ready for nine o'clock Mass. I don't think my parents have ever missed Mass in their entire lives. If we have to go on a trip or if we're out of town, they'll make plans to go to the Saturday Mass or else look everywhere for a Catholic church before we can do anything else. I have distinct memories of being five years old and walking around lost in Hong Kong while Mom and Dad asked directions to the nearest Catholic church. We missed a whole day at the Ocean Park roller coasters because of The Lord.

My parents aren't religious fanatics. They don't speak in tongues or shake tambourines and sing with their eyes closed or anything. In fact, some of Mom's (very distant) relatives are of the revivalist-percussionist strain, and for my grandfather's funeral, they had planned a special performance. But Mom wouldn't hear of it. "No one's banging on a bongo drum anywhere near my father's coffin!" she said.

Our car doesn't have a Jesus fish on it, and I don't own a "WWJD" bracelet (although secretly, I think they are kind of cute). We did watch *The Passion*, but Brittany cried so much that we had to turn it off. (Oh well, we all knew how it ends anyway.) In Manila every Lent the TV stations don't show anything but *The Ten Commandments* with Charlton Heston. As practicing Catholics, we attend Mass regularly. In the Philippines, everyone attends Mass on Sundays. Friends say to each other, "I'll pray for you" and it doesn't sound corny or pious.

Here in America there are Christian rock groups and Christian band camps and Christian cable networks. But for all the religious talk, it seems the only person who attends church is the President. And even then, it looks like he's only doing it for the cameras. But back home, we bumped into everyone at church: relatives, friends, Mom's socialite cronies, Dad's business associates, and customers from the restaurant. It was just another thing you did, like going to the country club on Saturdays.

No one at Grosvernor goes to church—at least that I know of.

Dr. Avilla asked me to tutor Whitney and Georgia last week, and they asked when we could get together to go over the English exam. Stupidly, I told them I was free Friday night. They snickered and said, what about Sunday morning instead? But I told them I couldn't, since I had to go to church. They both rolled their eyes and I knew they thought I was such a goody-goody.

I'm not. I don't even like going to church.

Okay, maybe I do. It's the only time other than geometry class that I get to see B-O-Y-S. You have to take what you can get when you go to an all-girls school. Plus, church is the only time I can dress up, so on Sundays I throw my own personal fashion show.

Which is why I was late today.

I couldn't decide what to wear. Plus, I was dreading having to see the Dalugdugans later. I knew why Mom was so keen on having them over, and I did not—repeat, did not—want to have to go through with it. I was still hoping she would give up on the idea of Freddie being my date for the Soirée. But I know Mom. She's persistent and she's got it in her head that this Soirée thing is really important to "assimilating."

Anyway, I have to wear a uniform five days a week. Do I wear the gray skirt or the gray skirt? The burgundy sweater or the burgundy blazer? (We were allowed to switch off, although most of us wore the blazer only on the required Mondays for Headmaster's Meeting.) Knee-high socks or knee-high socks?

Oh, the choices! So on weekends, when I'm free to wear whatever I like, I make the most of it. At the cafeteria on Saturday, I wear jeans and sneakers because I'm on my feet all day. But on Sundays, I bust out what I like to call "The Outfits."

I'm very serious about "The Outfits." I plan them days in advance in my head, coordinating shirts and skirts, colors and fabrics, deciding whether to go with trends or classics, plain-fronts or pleats. But this Sunday, I had no clue. I just didn't know what to wear. For a while, I had taken to throwing my thrift-store blazers over Dad's old tuxedo pants, which had gotten too small for him. I hemmed the bottoms to capri length and wore them with an old Lacoste shirt I had found crumpled up in the corner of the Gros locker room one day. But I was tired of doing that look.

I took out everything I owned from my closet and tried stuff on: my shrunken T-shirts; my favorite jeans; my camouflage pants; my furry sweater; my itchy sweater; my holey sweater; a houndstooth vintage suit I'd found at the Salvation Army for five bucks that reminded me of something Madonna would wear, the dreaded 49ers jacket.

But everything made me look fat, or short, or just didn't give me a good vibe.

"V, we're almost ready to go!" Mom called from downstairs half an hour before departure time.

I put on my standard backup ensemble: black sweater, black pants, and black flats. I looked in the mirror and saw a mime. Ugh. No.

"VICENZA! Let's go!" That was warning number two. Which meant I had five more minutes.

I ripped through the stack of clothes on my bed, slipping in and out of khakis, corduroys, denim, cotton, silk, wool, and rayon. I looked in the mirror, sucked in my cheeks, pursed my lips, and held my breath. Nothing.

"MARIA VICENZA ARAMBULLO!!!" That was DEFCON warning number three. Which meant we were in the danger zone—that there was a chance we wouldn't arrive in time to get our favorite seat—the first pew.

I quickly put on the new miniskirt that I had saved up for, thinking I would just wear it over my black tights and that would be fine. I walked down the stairs, grabbing my jean jacket and ran into Mom, who was standing by the staircase, her eyebrows raised.

"What are you wearing?"

"Huh?" I looked down. Did I have a run in my tights?

"You can't wear that to church! *Dios ko*, do you want to give the priest a heart attack?"

"What's wrong with it?"

"Your skirt! It's too short! Show some respect!"

"It's not too short! And I'm wearing tights!"

"Don't talk back to me!"

"But, Mom!"

"No! You have to change! Hurry. We're already late!"

"Mom!"

"PSSSSTTT!!!" She waved an angry finger and pointed to my room.

I stomped back upstairs, my heart black with hatred. I took off the miniskirt, grabbed the nearest pair of jeans, slipped them on, kicking off my treasured pair of black patent leather Mary Janes, and ran back downstairs. The house was empty since everybody was already in the Tan Van, and Dad already had the engine running.

"Ano ba? Bakit ang tagal?" Dad asked, looking over his shoulder at me. (What took you so long?)

I was puffing as I scooted in and slammed the door. I shrugged and looked away, blinking back tears. Life was so unfair. I couldn't even wear my new miniskirt to church! Where was God at this time?

Everyone else in my family was well turned out and nattily dressed. Dad had his "Regis Philbin" tie and matching jewel-colored shirt on under his lone sports jacket, Mom had on a silk blouse, pearls, and nice black slacks, and Brittany was wearing an adorable sailor dress. She kicked the back of Mom's seat absentmindedly, and for once Mom turned around with an irritated look on her face to tell her to stop. I slumped in the back, in my jean jacket and sneakers and uncombed hair, hating them all.

Our parish church is Our Lady of Sorrows, which is appropriate enough, since many parishioners are Filipinos in what my parents call "reduced circumstances" like us, as well as a sprinkling of Irish families. Mom and Dad walked all the way up to the first pew, where the Dalugdugans were already sitting. Mom gave them a strained smile, and Dad ushered us reluctantly into the second pew. Freddie winked at me and I grimaced. He was wearing a Montclair Academy varsity letter jacket, but he's no athlete. He's the manager of the lacrosse team. That one game I was able to attend, I saw Freddie on the bench, keeping score and statistics and handing out water and towels to the players between breaks.

I asked Dad once why we had to go to church, and he said because we are part of a community. I told him I thought church was boring and I didn't choose the faith, it was chosen for me. Surprisingly enough, he didn't argue with me. He said I might feel different when I grew up, but right now, I lived in their house and I had to follow their rules.

The reason my family likes to sit in the first pew is because whoever sits in the first pew gets to take up the wine and wafers at the Processional Offering before Communion. I saw Freddie's Dad get the nod from Mang Amoy, the gray-haired usher with the bad comb-over who smelled like cough drops. Sure enough, just as the choir burst into, "Yahweh, I know, you are near . . ." all three of the Dalugdugans stood up and walked slowly down the aisle to the little table holding two silver bowls and a crystal decanter of wine.

Until my family arrived to challenge them, the Dalugdugans always brought up the offering at the nine o'clock Mass. I watched them walk up together, reeking of smug, pleasant self-satisfaction. Freddie's dad, in his shiny sharkskin suit and Brylcreem in his pompadour; his mom, shuffling up in a beige crepe dress and plastic beads; and Freddie himself, the pride of Daly City.

I dozed off during the sermon, then played a game of thumb war with Brittany under the wrathful eye of my mother. Brit was always easy to distract. I made faces at her when my parents' backs were turned. As far as I was concerned, Communion was the most exciting part of Mass. It was a great people-watching spectacle. I craned my neck to see if my favorite church boy was there today. He was a tall Irish guy who always dressed in a button-down shirt and pressed khaki pants. But as the people passed us by, I didn't see him. The congregation at nine o'clock Mass was so regular, so punctual, that everyone would notice your absence or that of a member of your family. The Tuazons, for instance, were one person short, since Amelia was off at college; and Mrs. O'Shaughnessy's dentist husband had left her for his hygienist so she attended Mass alone.

When it was our turn to stand, I felt none of my usual excitement. This was a chance to show off my clothes, but since I hadn't been allowed to wear The Outfit, I merely slouched forward. I bent my head and clambered over Brittany, who had yet to take her First Communion. The holy wafer stuck to the top of my mouth, and I had to pry it off discreetly with my tongue. Like Mom and Dad, I hurried past the goblet of wine. Too many cooties. I couldn't imagine drinking from the same cup as a hundred other people.

As I knelt down, I prayed the same prayer I prayed every Sunday: *Please, Lord, let me have a boyfriend. Claude Caligari would be nice. Please, Lord, I can't be a teenager and never been kissed or never have a boyfriend. Please, Lord, let me have a cute date for the Gros Soirée so I can be normal. Please, please, please.*

When Mass was over, Mom and Dad made the rounds at church, greeting the priests and mingling with a few of their friends. They had maintained an aloof distance from the large Filipino community when we first arrived. "We didn't move to America just so we could hang out in Davao," Mom had sniffed. Mom and Dad took a lot of pride in Mom's Norwegian ancestry and Dad's Spanish surname.

The Dalugdugans certainly didn't look like any of Mom and

Dad's old friends back home—Mom's best friend Tita Kikit used to model in Singapore and had married an Austrian businessman, while Dad's social network was composed mainly of Spanish mestizos with blond children. But what Freddie's parents lacked in glamour, they more than made up for in kindness. They were guarantors on our lease; they had helped Dad rent office furniture and had introduced him to Mr. Bullfinch, the manager of the Sears department store, who was a client of theirs.

We met them through Mom's old nanny. Mom practically fell over in joy when she spotted *Manang* Toneng praying by the altar at church one day. It was a tearful reunion. Toneng had moved to America twenty years ago, but she and my grandmother had kept in touch over the years. Her daughter, Annabelle Ocampo, was the mayor of Daly City. Everyone at church was really impressed that we knew them. The Dalugdugans were good friends of theirs and took us under their wing immediately.

I had Freddie's parents to thank for my life at Gros, since they were the ones who told my parents that it was the sister school of Montclair Academy, where Freddie was a student. Grosvernor was the "best all-girls private school in San Francisco" according to his mom. It was also the most expensive. My parents spent their life savings paying for Brittany and me to attend, even with the scholarship money.

* * *

The church served coffee and bibingka after service, so everyone gathered in the vestry to snack and gossip. I wandered at the fringes of my parents' conversations, bored and picking at the sticky rice dessert in my hand. I wish the priests would just serve doughnuts.

"V, did you say hi to Tito Ebet and Tita Connie?" Mom asked, steering me to the Dalugdugans.

"Hi," I said, kissing both wanly on their cheeks. I liked them well enough, but I knew what Mom was planning and I didn't want anything to do with it.

"Since they're coming over for lunch, we should go home so we can get the Bean Dip ready," Mom said as she pulled me aside.

Somehow, Mom had gleaned that the proper food to serve while watching a football game consisted of six-foot submarine sandwiches, a tub of homemade guacamole, and something called Bean Dip. (When Mom said it, you could tell it had capital letters—it was that important.) We had never had any of this food before, and Mom was nervous about its preparation.

We rarely entertained, so it was a big deal, even if it was just Freddie and his dorky family. But my parents had insisted they come over, since the Dalugdugans had been nice enough to invite us to their house to watch the football game last week. We had sat in front of their sixty-inch projection television in awe.

We had no idea what any of the rules were or what was going on, but we cheered whenever they cheered, and we watched intently as Tita Connie prepared the famed Bean Dip.

Mom asked for the recipe, and I knew she was eager to show Tita Connie she could be as American as they were.

"Wanna ride?" Freddie asked, nudging me with his Styrofoam coffee cup.

"Mom! Can I go with Freddie?"

"What? Why?" I could tell she was annoyed that I was skipping out on her, but I didn't want to be stuck at home making sandwiches. I'd had enough of that at the cafeteria. Besides, maybe if I went with Freddie I could lie to Mom later and tell her he had turned me down.

"*Hindi na bali*, let the kids go," Tita Connie said, so my mom had to agree.

"I didn't know you had a *kotse*," I said, following Freddie to his car, a green Honda compact.

"We bought it last week. It's used," he said apologetically. "But it only has forty thousand miles on it. Not bad."

Freddie zapped his keys at the car, which made a beeping noise and flashed its lights. The doors automatically unlocked and we got in.

The dashboard was covered with a piece of cardboard made to resemble a giant pair of sunglasses. Inside the car were furry dice, a dancing Hawaiian girl, and a VIP ON BOARD sign in the back. Cheesy. Taped to the dashboard was a picture of a pretty Filipino girl in a pink ballgown with a beauty pageant crown on her head.

"*Sino yan?*" I pointed. (Who's that?)

He smiled mysteriously. "*Wala.*" (Nobody.)

Hmmm. Did Freddie have a girlfriend? Impossible. Just look at him. The glasses. The acne. The ninety-pound skeletal frame. I was mildly intrigued, but not really. I was still wishing Mom wouldn't make me do what she had bullied me into agreeing to do. It was the reason she had invited the Dalugdugans in the first place. But maybe she would forget all about it.

As we drove off from church, Freddie blasted Ludacris from the stereo system and flipped open the sunroof. He took a pack of cigarettes from the glove compartment and shook out a butt.

"Smoke?"

"No thanks."

He lit it with the car lighter and blew a puff out the window.

I didn't know Freddie smoked! Maybe under that Asian-Einstein exterior, he was actually a rebel. Then he began to cough and sputter. He stubbed the cigarette out in the ashtray.

"How's Gros?"

"Eh." I shook my head. "It's okay."

"Thought I saw you at Monty the other day."

"Yeah, I have geometry there now." I told him about the geometry chair scandal. He laughed.

"Who's in your class?"

I rattled off a couple of names and then offhandedly added, "Oh, and, um, Claude Caligari." It was a treat just saying his name aloud.

"Yeah, I know Claude. We're on the lacrosse team together."

Right, if you count fetching him a towel being on the team together, I thought.

"He's my study partner," I said dreamily.

"You should help him. He's flunking. It's not good for the team and we have State coming up."

Ludacris ended and Freddie put in a new CD. The Backstreet Boys' *The Hits: Chapter One*. I kid you not. He sang along to "I Want It That Way," "Quit Playing Games with My Heart," and "As Long as You Love Me" with gusto. He knew all the words. I was right. Freddie was still a geek.

The house smelled like rotten eggs, otherwise known as Mrs. Dalugdugan's Famous Football-Watching Party Bean Dip. The "game" was on TV, but we had already missed kickoff. Freddie and I grabbed a few sandwiches from the table and sat on the floor.

Of course, when we arrived, the first thing Mom said was

"Vicenza, did you ask Freddie yet?"

"Ask me what, Tita Didi?" he asked, his mouth full of salami.

"Nothing," I mumbled.

"Go ahead, don't be shy. Girls are so modest!" Tita Connie said, as she scooped up a hefty portion of dip with a large nacho chip. Tita Connie was so corny. She called dating "courtship" and once asked me in all sincerity if anyone was "wooing" me now that I was all grown up and in high school. Seriously! It made my skin crawl. Tita Connie and Mom smiled at each other.

Freddie nudged me. *"Ano?"*

"D'youhafadatefortheMontyGrosSoirée," I said, looking down at my paper plate.

Freddie chewed for a couple of minutes, then said, "No."

"Dyouwanttogowithmethen?"

"Okay." Freddie shrugged, his eyes fixed on the television.

"What did he say?" Mom asked, peering down at us.

"He said yes, Mom."

"How nice!" Mom beamed. Tita Connie positively glowed. I wanted to slap the grins off their faces.

"It's in December, right?" Freddie asked.

"Yeah. Mom really wants me to go. You don't have to if you don't want to," I whispered.

"I've never been, so okay, *lang* . . ." (It's fine.)

"Okay."

I felt bad about not wanting to go with Freddie, since he was being so cool about it. But I just didn't want to show up with him on my arm, although it didn't seem like I had a choice. Mom was really determined that I should go and experience "everything an American high school has to offer."

Isobel would kill me when she finds out I wimped out on our pact.

"TOUCHDOWN!!!!" We all looked up to see Tito Ebet and my dad high-five each other as the Niners scored their first goal.

I didn't know Dad knew how to do the Touchdown Boogie.

PEACHES!!

The BEST news all year! I have a date for the Soirée! Claude is taking me to the dance! I asked him when we were watching the Niners game at his house. He was, like, No, I should ask YOU to the Soirée. And then he did, and of course, I said YES.

I think Whit was a little weird about it, but she's still hot and heavy with her boyfriend from Carmel, so I don't think it matters. Why does she want ALL the boys? I just want ONE.

Miss you,

V

BTW—That's so great that your family might come visit San Francisco this Christmas! Let me know EXACTLY when you guys are planning to get here so we can hang out with Whitney and all of my friends!

11

But Is It a Date-Date?

FOR DAYS AFTERWARD, Mom and Tita Connie kept calling each other because they were so excited Freddie and I were going to the dance together. It was truly depressing. I didn't tell Isobel because I was embarrassed to have broken our pact so quickly. For once, I was glad to be at the safe haven of the Sears cafeteria in the afternoons.

"Um, what does a guy have to do to get a Pepsi around here?"

I looked up from my book and saw Paul standing in front of me. I hadn't even noticed. I yawned and looked at the clock. Fifteen minutes to six. I would be able to close the cafeteria soon. "Hey, haven't seen you all week," I said. "Where have you been hiding?"

"I broke up with Laurie, so I wanted to lay low."

I was so clueless, I didn't even know he was even dating anybody. I felt my stomach clench. Laurie had big hair and plastic earrings. She wore her jeans so low, her thong peeked out when she bent over. She ordered chili dogs and nachos. She had long, press-on nails that she liked to drum on the counter while she decided between Diet Pepsi or bottled water. She never tipped.

"How long were you guys dating?"

"Not too long—like, a month." He shrugged.

"What happened?"

"I dunno."

"You don't seem so worked up about it."

"Nah, not really. But whatever. How've you been?"

"Okay," I said.

"How's that doofy school you go to?"

"Sucks."

"Figures."

"How's your band?"

He smiled. "Not bad. Most of the time everyone just goofs off. Buncha jokers," he said affectionately. "We're trying to get something together to make a CD. A friend of mine has this whole setup on his computer where we can produce our own record."

"Wow."

"Yeah, it's pretty crazy what you can do with computers now."

"Oh, I have your book. The, um, Stephen King? I read it," I said. I took it out from my backpack and handed it to him.

"And?"

"It was great. I loved it. I got a couple more." I showed him what I was reading—the newest Dark Tower book.

"Really?" He grinned slyly. "I told you! But you shouldn't have spent your money. And you should start with the first one. I can lend you my copy."

"It's okay. I borrowed them all from the library."

"Man, you are so square it's cute."

I felt my cheeks flush. I loved the South San Francisco library. It was another thing my family couldn't believe about America—books on loan! For free! Dad said if they had a library like that in the Philippines, all the books would be stolen in a day.

Every week, my family makes a special trip to pick out books. It was another of our nerdy habits I tried to keep people at Gros from knowing about. The library had a lot of Stephen King books, but I also wanted my own copies of my favorites. I liked seeing them lined up on my bookshelves, easily within reach if I wanted to reread them. Books borrowed from the library were valued but ephemeral pleasures.

"Hey, you know they made a movie out of the latest Stephen King book? Usually they're kind of terrible, but who knows— maybe they got it right this time," he said, raising his eyebrows so high his shoulders peaked, too.

"Probably not. Those things always suck," I said.

"Yeah, but there's *The Shining*. Or *Misery*. You never know, this one could be good."

"I guess." I shrugged.

"I saw the trailer—it looks awesome. This guy's head explodes and it's, like, filled with this mucky green stuff that glows and, like, takes over. Bitchin'."

I made a face. "Is it scary?"

"Of course it's scary. Isn't that the point?" He looked impatient. "So, you, like, don't want to see it?"

"I dunno. I really haven't thought about it."

"Well, it's opening next Friday. Maybe you'll change your mind."

"Oh, all right," I said, before I even knew what I was saying.

"Great!" he said, beaming at me. Then his face fell. "I forgot—that weekend, I might have to visit my dad in Fresno."

"Why? What's he doing there?"

"He lives there. My parents are divorced."

"Oh, I'm sorry—about your parents, I mean," I said kind of awkwardly.

"Don't be. It's a lot better for everyone."

I didn't know anyone who was divorced. None of my parents' friends was divorced. Divorce was illegal in the Philippines, so nobody got divorced. At least, not in Manila. Couples traveled to the United States or Hong Kong to get divorced. But there were a lot of "second families" and "Manila wives" (meaning, there were other wives stashed away somewhere else).

"Is it hard, with him away?"

He looked startled that I was asking so many questions.

"A little, yeah. I miss him. It's weird. But I get to see him one weekend each month, and I live up there during the summer."

"The whole summer?"

"Yeah, it's cool. Dad pretty much lets me do what I want."

I felt a little sad thinking Paul wouldn't be around in the summer. I knew where I would be: here at the cafeteria making sandwiches, running the register, counting out change.

"So, do you want to go see it together? Um, unless, you know, you're busy."

I was so far from busy it was ridiculous. "Sure, why not?"

"I can meet you at the theater. It's playing in the mall."

"Sure."

"Do you have a cell number? I can call you so we can hook up."

I gave him my number on the back of an old receipt.

"All right then." He paid me for his Pepsi and walked out of the cafeteria. I waved at him when he looked back through the door's porthole.

I was smiling so hard my mouth hurt. I still didn't quite know what happened. Did he just ask me out? Did we have a date? Or was it a friendly thing? I mean, he just broke up with

Laurie, whom I didn't even know he was dating! Maybe I was just his, like, cafeteria buddy. But what did I care anyway? It wasn't like I *liked*-him-liked-him.

In any case, I would have to find some way to go to the movies with him. My parents would never allow it. Not that they had anything against him, but it was just part of the rules. My fifteenth birthday was still a month away.

The next day at school I told Isobel about Paul.

"This guy—a, um, friend of mine, kinda asked me to go the movies with him next Friday."

"Really! What does he look like?"

"Skinny. Tall." What did Paul look like? "He has brown hair and green eyes and kind of a small mouth, but I think it's because of the braces. He has a nose that kind of looks like it's been broken, and he has freckly arms and knobby wrists. . . ."

"Whoa—didn't need the entire four-one-one, I meant, is he cute?"

Was Paul cute? I guess some people might think so. The girls at Sears certainly did. "Yeah I guess . . . but he listens to Incubus."

"*Quoi?*"

"It's a heavy metal band," I explained.

"Ah! *Je connais. Comme* 'Headbangers Ball.' So is it love?" she teased.

"No, we're just friends."

"*Bon.*"

"Do you think it's a date?"

"Of course it's a date," she said as she tried, and failed, to slam her locker door. She kept a mini clothes closet in there, and her wardrobe was always threatening to tumble out in an explosion of pink leather and gold sequins.

"How do you know?" I asked, helping her smoosh in all her clothes and marveling at a Lycra T-shirt with fishnet sleeves that read J'ADORE DIOR in an allover pattern.

"He asked you, didn't he?"

"Yeah, so . . ."

"So nothing. It's a date," she declared, snapping the lock closed and pulling up her black spandex capri leggings underneath her uniform skirt. Next to Whitney, Isobel was always out of uniform. Unlike Whitney, Isobel was always in detention for it. "Who's this guy again?"

"Paul Hartwell. I told you about him before. He works at Sears. He goes to public school. He's nice," I said, trying to play it down. "But, I don't know, we're friends."

"*Très* simple. Guys aren't friends with girls." She considered herself an expert in boy-girl relations since she was still conducting a lame long-distance relationship with Sam in New York, even if they both knew it was over. He had stopped IM-ing her every night, and every time she called his dorm room, his room-mate said he was out.

"Observe it this way, V. Do you have any guy friends?"

I thought about Freddie—but he was more a family friend than a personal one. As for Paul, I definitely thought of him as a friend—nothing more. I kind of hoped it *wasn't* a date.

"Let's talk about this later," I said. "I'm late for geometry."

"Is that boy still in your class?" she asked.

"Who?" I asked. "Oh, you mean Claude. Yeah, he's still there. Not doing too well though. We get our midterms back today. I think I passed but only thanks to you, Iz."

I walked quickly into Montclair, following a couple of sopho-mores in my class and ignoring the curious looks girls always received from the boys there. Some of the guys were total jerks—they'd always wolf whistle or pound their chests and say "hubba hubba" or stick their tongues out lecherously—but lately they've gotten used to our presence. Once when they teased us about being "geometry whores" Stacey Bennett slugged one of the boys in the nose. They stopped bothering us after that.

The first bell rang when I was still in the hallway, and when I arrived in class, Miss Tresoro was already handing out the results of midterms.

I took my seat and looked at the stapled graph paper that was lying facedown in front of my desk. The rules of my scholarship dictated I had to keep an A minus average, and I had A's in all my other classes, but to keep an A minus, I need to pull at least a B in geometry.

Isobel had been nice enough to spend every lunch hour and free period tutoring me, and I felt confident I had done a little better. But I was still scared. My parents would kill me if I lost my scholarship.

I turned over my test.

B. GREAT IMPROVEMENT was scrawled on the top of the page. Thank God!

"That's awesome," Claude said, seeing my grade.

"Thanks." I smiled, forgetting that I was too intimidated to talk to him.

"Here—you turn it over," he said, pushing his test over to my side of the table. "I don't even wanna know."

"Are you sure?" I asked.

"Yep. Do it."

I turned over his test.

"What does it say?" he asked.

I showed him.

Another F. PLEASE SEE ME Miss Tresoro had written in big block letters.

He cursed vehemently under his breath.

"I'm sorry," I whispered.

"How'd you get so good? You weren't doing that much better than me before."

I nodded. "My friend Isobel—the one you hit with your car?—she's, like, a math genius. She's been helping me with my homework."

"Do you think she could do the same for me, even though I almost killed her?" Claude asked.

Isobel tutor Claude? I felt a stab of jealousy. But he looked so forlorn, with none of his usual swagger. "Sure, I'll ask her. What time do you have lunch tomorrow?"

"Umm . . . G period," he said after consulting his Palm Pilot.

"Ours is, too. You know that French bistro on Fillmore?" It was Isobel's favorite café. She said it reminded her of home.

"Yeah, the one with the black-and-white awning?"

"Meet us there at one, and don't forget to bring your geometry book," I said.

The next day, I was so excited for our lunchtime appointment, I kept reapplying my lipstick and tried to do something about my hair. Isobel pretended not to care, but I noticed she had put more blush on her cheeks than usual and had hiked up her skirt two more rolls over the waistband so it was practically nonexistent. I didn't really mind that there would be three of us. It was my first official date with Claude Caligari!

FROM: queen_vee@aol.com

TO: amparo.dellarosa@info.ph.com

SENT: Thursday, November 12, 9:55 PM

SUBJECT: finally alone!!

Today Claude and I met for coffee at this really cute French café down the street. He's so cute. Like me, he reads all the time. We're both total bookworms. We have so much in common. We both ordered mocha cappuccinos.

I'm so sorry to hear you and Rufi broke up! But at least your parents never found out about it.

I can't wait for you to get here in December! It turns out Whitney and everyone will be away for break, so you won't be able to meet them. :-(

Love,

V, AKA Mrs. Caligari

12

Cinderella Problems

SOBEL IS NOW tutoring Claude and me during every free period. While things at school were looking up, back at the cafeteria, I didn't see Paul for a couple of days, which was kind of disappointing. I was looking forward to seeing the movie with him, even if I knew it really wasn't a date. I figured he'd probably forgotten all about it, so I was happily surprised when he called me on my cell Tuesday afternoon.

"Hello?"

"Hey, V, it's me, Paul."

"Oh, hi!" I said, turning away so Mom, who was in the Toyota with me, wouldn't hear.

"Where are you guys? It's not even five o'clock."

I explained that Mom and I had closed the cafeteria a little earlier for a special errand.

"Can you check the map again?" she asked, peering over the steering wheel as we drove off the highway into the warehouse district. "Who's that on the phone?"

"No one," I mouthed, a little embarrassed that I was talking to a boy on the phone, even if it was just Paul.

"Hold on," I told him. "It says Fourth Street and Divisadero, Mom," I said, consulting a faded San Francisco street map. "Oh, there it is."

"My dad canceled on me this weekend, so do you want to see that Stephen King movie this Friday?" he asked.

"Sure," I said.

"Cool. Should I pick you up?"

I laughed. Why was he being so formal? "I can just meet you there," I said, hoping to be as evasive as possible since I didn't want Mom to know I was making plans to meet a boy. I still didn't know exactly how I was going to be able to sneak out to the movies with him.

"Cool. There's, like, a little fountain in front that we can meet at," he said.

"Okay, see you then. Bye."

"Later."

I was glad Mom was too busy parking to pay much attention. "Ayayay! Look at that line," she said, clicking her tongue.

The line in front of the Jessica McClintock outlet store was so long, we had to stand several blocks away from the entrance when we finally arrived. Several women were armed with folding chairs, bottled water, and decks of cards.

"Are they actually letting people in?" an elegant lady behind us asked.

"I've been here since noon. It's worse than a concert," replied a dark-haired girl with a tongue ring.

It was Mom's idea to hit the outlet to buy me a dress for the Soirée. She clutched the extra-ten-percent-off coupon she had clipped from the newspaper and kept checking to see it was still in her pocket.

"Stop it, Mom. Let me hold it," I said, a little annoyed by her fidgeting.

"Okay," she said, handing it to me.

But that didn't work, because then every ten seconds she asked, "You still have the coupon, right, V? Right?"

"Yes, I still have the coupon. What's the big deal? It's only ten percent off!" I said huffily.

"Don't talk back to me that way," Mom said. "Is that what you're learning in school? To talk back to your parents?"

I looked down at the ground and said nothing. Mom was really getting on my nerves. She was in my face so much—asking me too many questions, forever getting on me about my clothes, my multiple Tobey Maguire posters on the wall ("The tape will ruin the wallpaper! And we won't get our security deposit back!" she'd warned me direly). The other day she interrogated me on why I was wearing a blue sweater to school instead of my usual cranberry one. Like everyone in my class, I had begun to wear a blue sweater like the one only allowed to seniors because Whitney had started doing so. But it's not like Mom would understand if I told her why.

"You used to tell me everything," she lamented. It was something she said so often it had become a refrain. "You used to tell me everything, now all you do is talk on the phone to that French girl or else you're online e-mailing Peaches."

Mom had been very close to her mother, and I knew it disappointed her that I wasn't her best friend. Mom's argument is that there wasn't a "generation gap" between us since she was only twenty-six when I was born. But Mom just doesn't get it. Sometimes, it seems that she grew up in the fifties, not the eighties. Mom told me that when Dad was "courting her" (her words, not mine!) Dad would come over and have dinner with the family before they could go out together. They'd met in a Christmas caroling group in college—how *7th Heaven* is that?

"I'm sorry, Mom," I said. "I just wish this line wasn't so long."

"Me, too." She sighed.

I was excited to see what they had in stock. Even if I had to go with Freddie, I was still looking forward to getting all done up for the big night. Mom had promised to bring me to the beauty salon to get my hair blow-dried. She cut my hair herself, but she was so excited for my "first American dance" that she said this time I could get Manang Charing at Marikit Beauty Parlor in Daly City to give me a wash and dry.

When we lived in Manila, every Saturday, Mom took me with her to her weekly visit to Arthur at his salon. Arthur was the *ne plus ultra* (I learned how to say that from Isobel) of hair. He was the man behind Imelda Marcos's bouffant, and when we arrived at his pink-marble-and-fuchsia-draped salon, he showered Mom with a flutter of air kisses, screeching, *"Mrs. Didi!! Kamusta na! Ang ganda mo naman! Ang galing ko talaga!"* in the same breath complimenting my mother on her beauty while also congratulating himself for his excellent work.

Next to grandma, Mom probably missed Arthur the most. Because when we moved to San Francisco, Mom had to learn how to give herself manicures, as well as how to cut everyone in the family's hair. When Dad got a five-dollar haircut from a Chinatown barber, he returned looking like a plucked chicken. After that, Mom bought a learning video and a pair of professional shears. It wasn't hard to approximate Arthur's bowl cuts on Brittany, and Dad mostly just needed a trim, but I often emerged from the family beauty salon looking a little . . . well, strange. Somehow, my requests to look more like Reese Witherspoon would always turn me into a miniature Kelly Osbourne. Mom picked on me about my hair, but really it was her fault.

The line at the outlet finally began to move, and we shuffled along the sidewalk following the rest of the bargain-hunting hordes. I was suddenly struck by how familiar the line seemed—the orderly procession tinged with anticipation and a dash of desperation. Where had I seen this before? Then I remembered. It was just like the line at the Homeland Security and Immigration office, where we went when we first arrived in the country, in the summer. Dad had to ask a question about our green card applications. Apparently, to actually talk to an INS official, Dad would have to be one of the first fifty people in line. The Dalugdugans advised us to get there as early as possible, since most people started lining up for an appointment at two in the morning. We all bundled up and drove to downtown San Francisco at midnight. My parents decided to take the whole family because even though I argued that I was old enough, they didn't feel comfortable leaving us at home alone, and they didn't know anyone well enough to trust them to baby-sit.

We sat on the sidewalk with all the other beige- and brown-skinned immigrants (if there was a white person there, I didn't see one). The line hummed with the friendly, tumultuous babble of various languages, and a certain we're-all-in-this-together camaraderie began to develop. I noticed that people would hold each other's place in line politely if you asked, for instance, if you had to run to the twenty-four-hour Wendy's across the street to use the bathroom. Most people spent the night telling each other their stories. We made friends with a Mexican family who shared their homemade tortillas with us and told us about how they smuggled themselves across the border in the trunk of a Lincoln Continental. We gave them a few rolls of pan de sal Mom had made the day before.

At the head of the line were two INS security guards who dozed off intermittently. When they were awake, they tried to keep everyone's spirits up. When a family of five arrived at half-past two, the guards told them they were too late to be one of the first fifty appointments. They took it hard, grumbled a little, and said they would return the next day.

The INS office opened at seven A.M., and we all watched the sun rise above the Bank of America tower and the Transamerica building. A few coffee and doughnut vendors rolled up with their carts, and people started yawning, stretching, and unzipping their sleeping bags. We shuffled in through the glass doors, through the metal detectors, and were finally allowed inside the building.

Once inside, there were even more lines ahead. There was a line for every possible predicament: one for people who were picking up new green cards, another for people who had lost their existing green cards, and yet another line for people who were asking questions about their current green-card applications. And the longest line was for people who didn't have green cards at all. When we were finally in the right line, we were ushered into a large, dimly lit room the size of a football field, with neat, plastic orange chairs arranged in a row and flashing digital monitors hanging from the ceiling that blinked your ticket number. We each sat on one of these chairs and every time someone got called, you moved over to the next chair, then the next.

For Dad's one question, we had to wait for nine hours, not counting the five hours we spent outside.

And Dad thought the DMV was bad.

"Can I see your invitation?" a bored salesclerk asked when we finally arrived at the front of the line at the outlet store.

"Excuse me, our invitation?" Mom asked, waving her ten-percent-off coupon.

"Can't you read? Today's sale is invitation only. It's not open to the public until tomorrow." She pointed at the small print at the bottom of the coupon.

Mom peered at it. *Press preview and VIP sale on Tuesday, open to public on Wednesday*, it read. Of course, we didn't have an invitation to the sale.

"No, I'm sorry, we don't have an invitation, but my daughter and I have been waiting in line for two hours."

"Tough luck. Come back tomorrow."

I sighed and began to turn away, but Mom stood her ground.

"That isn't fair!" she said. "We have been waiting for so long. I'm sorry we made this mistake, but can't you make an exception? Why are you letting those people in?" she demanded, seeing the elegant woman and a Christina Aguilera clone being waved inside.

The stony-faced clerk glared. "They have VIP passes from the boutique."

"But we didn't know! This is an outrage!" Mom argued. "Can I see a manager?"

I was surprised at Mom's tenacity. She was usually so meek at a time like this. "Americans talk so quickly!" she always complained. "I can never understand what they're saying!" She always assumed such a humble air; I had forgotten how much attitude she could muster if needed. But nothing brought out the best in my mom like the possibility that she might miss a sale.

We were inside the outlet store in two minutes.

"Take the right side, I'll take the left!" Mom said, taking control of the situation. Divide and conquer was her preferred mode of operation during a big sale. She understood that speed was an important factor in successful outlet shopping—*grab first, check sizes later!*

I ran to the right, hoping to find the perfect gown. I had seen Nicole Kidman wearing a variation of my dream dress at the Oscars—something off the shoulder, slinky, and glittery—or maybe I could wear something short and sequiny and mod. I selected a few choices—a short black lace dress with rhinestone beading, a strapless silk sheath, a halter-top and skirt combo, and began to look for Mom on the other side of the room.

"Mom?" I asked a moving mountain of taffeta that was wearing my mother's familiar black pants. "Is that you under there?"

The taffeta rustled, so I took it as a yes.

Mom's face abruptly appeared at the top of the stack. She was breathing in short, staccato gasps, the way she does when she is very excited or nervous.

"What is that?" I asked, grimacing when I had a better look at the gowns she was holding.

"Found the clearance rack! Extra seventy percent off!" Mom smiled cheerfully. "Let's go to the dressing room and see how they fit!"

The dressing room was a large, cordoned-off section in the back filled with half-naked women struggling into formal wear. It lacked partitions or any semblance of privacy. I tried not to look at strangers in their underwear, their flesh bulging out from thongs and girdles. Mom and I are the type of people who hide behind bathroom stalls to change in the women's locker room.

I gave her a questioning look, and Mom shrugged.

I gingerly stepped out of my clothes and pulled the black lace dress over my head.

"That's nice," Mom said. She peered at the price tag. "*Ay*, not so nice."

I looked at it: $199. It was a steal, considering the original price was $899, but it was still out of our budget. I took it off reluctantly. Every dress I had chosen met the same fate—they looked perfect on me, but were way beyond our reach, pricewise. I felt my heart sink whenever Mom flipped up the price tag and sighed.

"But you have your coupon . . ." I said.

"Even at ten percent off, it's still too much. I'm sorry, baby. Try on the dresses I chose," she urged.

I looked dubiously at a pink-and-black strapless monstrosity she was holding. "I don't know about that, Mom. It's, like, *pink*."

"There's some black in it. C'mon try it. Look, it's only fifty dollars!" she said cheerfully. "With my coupon, that's forty-five dollars!"

I peeled off the backless black silk sheath, hung it up with much reluctance, and wriggled into the strapless taffeta, which was so starched and fussy, it was like sliding into a wedding cake. The dress was like a survivor from the *Footloose* prom set—a frilly nightmare with three layers of ruffles and a peplum waist. It wasn't so much designed as upholstered.

"What's that on the back?" I asked, turning to look at myself in the mirror, and finding a gigantic ribbon at the end of my back. "I don't know, Mom."

"I think you look beautiful!" Mom said. "So grown-up! And the waist is so flattering!"

I studied my image in the mirror critically. Oh well. I was going to the dance with Freddie, so who really cared what I looked like?

But the thing was, I did care. The dance was my one opportunity to get all dolled up and I had a vision of transforming myself into some kind of red-carpet goddess, wearing an outfit to end all outfits. Kind of like the way Renée Zellweger shows up to the Oscars looking fantastic after losing all the weight she had to gain for the Bridget Jones movies. "Look at your shoulders, they look so nice, and the pink brings out the color in your cheeks."

"I guess."

Who would look at my cheeks when there was an insanely huge bow on my ass?

"Do you like it?" Mom asked, looking at me so hopefully I thought I would cry.

I didn't like it. I hated it. It looked and felt cheap and tacky. But I didn't want to disappoint my mom. She had closed the cafeteria early just so we could get to the sale in time. She just wanted me to be happy, and I knew it would make her happy if

I lied. I figured at least one of us would be happy.

"I love it, Mom. It looks great."

"I knew it! I'm so good at knowing things! See, I know you so well. I knew you'd like it immediately." She began fussing with the dress, pulling it at the waist, at the hips, fluffing out the taffeta layers and humming to herself.

I felt utterly crushed. Even though I knew there was no way Freddie and I would ever be voted Soirée Roi and Reine, the dress killed every fantasy I had of arriving at the ball looking like one.

The saleslady put my dress in a garment bag, and Mom finally relinquished her coupon with gusto. "Let's tell Daddy!" Mom said, flipping open her cell phone. "Hi, honey . . . What?" She suddenly yelped. "Why? Oh no! What? So what will happen to us? *Bakit? Ay, Patay!*" She began to use words she had forbidden us to use in our house.

"What? What happened?" I asked, nervous to see her acting that way.

"Oh my God!" Mom said, putting a hand on her chest to steady herself. "The video store . . ."

"Yes . . . ??"

"It's been raided! Your cousin has been arrested for illegally renting tapes of American TV shows!"

FROM: queen_vee@aol.com

TO: amparo.dellarosa@info.ph.com

SENT: Tuesday, November 17, 8:15 PM

SUBJECT: The dress from hell!

Omigod! EMERGENCY! I got the ugliest dress for the
Soirée! Claude is going to laugh when he sees it! I begged
and begged and begged my mom to buy me something else,
but she wouldn't listen. So: okay, my dress is like a flashback
to the 80s. First of all, it has three layers of ruffles! It's like a
wedding cake! Worse, it's alternating—pink and black! So,
pink ruffle. Then black ruffle. Then pink ruffle. But wait—
the kicker—it's got a BUTT BOW!!! Omigod. Everyone from
Gros will be wearing slinky little Arden B sheaths and cute
little Tocca dresses and I'll be in a BUTT BOW!! I hate my
dress!! I hate it!! AGGHHH. I'M SO MISERABLE!!!!!

Okay, I just had to vent.

Love,

V

13
Hiding in the Bathroom
Isn't the Answer Either

THE NEWS WAS as bad as it sounded. When we got home, Dad was on the phone with Kuya Norbert, my cousin who ran the video store, who was calling from—of all places—jail.

Just the other month Norbert had sent us a video of his own. The tape showed him standing in front of what looked like any ordinary living room. "This is the back room of the store," Norbert had said. "Look, it's a fridge! Or is it?" he asked gleefully, as he opened the door to reveal that the appliance was filled with VHS tapes. I even recognized my handwriting on several of the cassettes.

Norbert was my mother's brother's eldest son and something of a cutup. He had spent his youth racing motorcycles and generally goofing off, but he'd suddenly developed an entrepreneurial streak when he settled down and got married. It was his idea to bring tapes of American reality TV shows to his customers, and the business was a hit. Copyright laws were being flouted everywhere in Asia. Peaches told me she had seen *Star Wars III* on DVD even before it hit the theaters. None of us thought taping TV shows would be a big deal.

Norbert's tour of the back room continued with the same cheerful reveal of each of the room's hidden storage areas. "Look a window!" he said, but when he pulled up the blinds, it was also stacked with cassettes. There was a false wall in the armoire, several secret compartments in the couch, and several more false windows. Norbert giggled, obviously tickled by the whole idea.

"*Gago!*" (foolish boy) Mom had said, bemused at the time.

Dad had shaken his head and grunted. I'd e-mailed Peaches, to tell her that the latest copy of *America's Top Weight-loss Secrets* should be on its way to Norbert's Spectacular Video Store in Makati.

It was all supposed to be so harmless.

"What's going to happen now?" I asked Dad.

He hung up the phone. "I don't know. I just called Tita Delia in Malacañang. Norbert's out on bail, but the charges are serious. It's a pretty big fine if he's convicted. They are beginning to crack down on a lot of things that they usually let slide. Hopefully it will all work out in the end. But we're not going to be taping shows for a while."

Mom's face was ashen. Her favorite nephew in trouble was bad enough, but now money was going to be a problem, too. The proceeds from our reality-TV VHS smuggling were small but substantial. "Next semester's tuition is due in a month," Mom whispered.

"We'll find a way. Maybe the JCPenney across the mall will let us open a cafeteria in their store," Dad said hopefully. So far, the other Sears stores in the Bay Area had proved immune to the charms of Arambullo Food Services.

I pretended not to hear and walked slowly up the stairs to my room, carrying my hated Soirée dress.

The next day, I stopped thinking about the video store's smuggling demise, Norbert's troubles with the law, and the problems with the cafeteria, since I had more important things to worry about, like a huge geometry exam. It was the last chance I had to pull up my grade before semester finals.

"I can't do this anymore." Claude groaned, banging his head on his open textbook. He looked so adorable, with his blond hair sticking up in tufts.

He looked up from the book, and Isobel and I burst into laughter. We were sitting in our favorite corner table of Bistro Felix during lunch. Claude was now a regular at our geometry study breaks. I'd asked Isobel if she minded, and at first the two of them were wary about each other but they had started to get along.

"It is imperative!" Isobel scolded. "The exam is next period!"

"You're getting better," I said to him. "You got problems one through ten right on the practice test."

"Yeah, but Izzy lets me cheat," he said, smiling at her.

Isobel smiled back, and I felt a little strange, sitting between them. Isobel knew I had a huge crush on Claude, and I also knew she would never do anything to compromise our friendship.

We were both advocates of the belief that *thou shalt not steal thy best friend's man*—even if it was just a crush. Certainly, Peaches and I never had those problems. Peaches was a Jake Gyllenhaal girl.

Not that it mattered anyway, since Claude was very much Whitney's new boyfriend. He always came by to pick her up after school, and the two of them had their arms around each other constantly. They looked so perfect together—they had the same shade of hair, and Whitney was almost as tall as Claude. They caused a slight commotion wherever they went. It was as if they were in perpetual lip lock—it made me feel sick.

Headmaster Humphrey had even warned the student body during Headmaster's Meeting about "inappropriate actions" on school grounds—the five-block area between Montclair and Grosvernor.

"There have been some, ahem, complaints. The Board of Trustees has received word about girls in Grosvernor uniforms smoking and engaging in questionable conduct around the city," he said, his lips forming a priggish little frown.

He looked straight down at where Whitney was sitting, but she didn't even squirm. She just looked back at him without blinking, chewing her gum and playing with her hair.

"Okay, concentrate. I give you five minutes to do the next problem. Then we take a cappuccino break," Isobel ordered.

"I'm done," Claude announced, lifting his pencil. "I think I got it right this time."

"Me, too," I said.

Isobel checked our pages warily. She pushed her cat's-eye glasses up her nose. "Hmmm . . . not bad, not bad . . . this one is a little off, but otherwise okay. . . ."

"What are you guys doing this Friday night?" Claude asked.

Isobel faked nonchalance, and I tried not to look too excited. We both knew he was having a huge party at his house that night. Whitney tortured the rest of the freshman class by constantly talking about it. Details had been leaked to weloveclaudecaligari.com, so I already knew all about it: they had gotten some famous nightclub guy to DJ, Claude's older brother was taking care of the keg, and his parents would be away in Mexico for the weekend.

"I might be going out . . ." Isobel said.

"Yeah, I think I have plans for Friday, too." I shrugged.

"Too bad. I'm having a party that night."

"Oh, yeah? Maybe we'll stop by." Isobel cocked an eyebrow. I looked nonchalant.

"Thirty-three Presidio, in Saint Francis Woods. Come anytime after eight," he said, scribbling his address on Isobel's notebook.

"Okay."

"See you then!"

"Later."

He loped off and met Whitney, who was waiting for him in front of the café and scowling at us through the window. We had overheard her calling us Claude's "loser girl study group" one day, but instead of being embarrassed, Isobel and I thought it was kind of funny, so we had taken to calling each other card-carrying members of the L.G.S.G. I think it bothered Whitney that there was nothing she could do to stop it, especially since she was failing algebra, so it's not as if she could help him with geometry. She broke into a smile when she saw Claude, who planted a huge sloppy kiss on her lips. Isobel and I traded disgusted looks.

After lunch I had gym class, which was held in the outdoor courtyard between the school buildings, which had ceased to be a minor annoyance and had become a full-blown nightmare. All week we were faced with the annual Presidential Fitness Challenge. Gros prided itself on having all its girls score in the top ninetieth percentile. But not if I had anything to do with it. So far, I had barely passed each activity. I nervously stood in line, waiting for the next torture, which was balance and coordination.

We'd each been given a paddle and a Ping-Pong ball, as well as a partner to document your progress. The object was to test your reflexes by bouncing the ball on the paddle twice.

After everyone paired up, I was left with Sylvia Abernofsky, a skinny girl with buck teeth. She completed the task after several tries. "Your turn," she said.

I put the ball on the paddle and flipped it.

The ball rocketed off the fence with a bang, almost hitting the second graders in the adjoining courtyard. "Sorry!" I said, as I ran over to retrieve it. On my second try, the ball rolled down to the basketball court. I started to feel increasingly uncomfortable as I repeatedly tried and failed to bounce that stupid Ping-Pong ball on the freaking paddle. The rest of the class had moved on to the sprint test.

"C'mon, Arambullo, hurry up, you can do it!" Miss Farnworthy, our gym teacher bellowed. She was a large, chesty woman with a loud voice and a blond afro, who usually gave me a break.

"I'm trying!" I said, once again flipping up the ball, only to swipe the air uselessly with my paddle.

"What a retard," I heard someone say clearly behind me.

I turned and looked Whitney Bertoccini straight in the eye.

She poised her ball on the paddle, gave it a small rap and bounced it up and down twice. "Done!" she said.

Unnerved, I tried again, but whatever I was doing, it wasn't right. I just couldn't bounce the ball. I would fail the Presidential Fitness exam, flunk gym class, and lose my academic scholarship. My parents would kill me. It was surreal.

"Don't worry about it," Sylvia whispered. "I'll just record that you did it."

"Okay." I nodded, thankful for her sympathy.

Miss Farnworthy and the rest of the class were already outside the school grounds running laps around the block so it was easy enough to lie. When they trooped in, Sylvia and I handed in our sheets. I followed everyone to the locker room to change, just in time to see Whitney flailing her arms and pretending to lunge for a ball with an invisible paddle.

"Omigod! Did it go up my skirt?" She snorted.

Georgia and Trish were in hysterics.

"I swear! Is there a bigger loser in the class?! I mean, how hard is it to hit a little ball?"

I backed out of the locker room and ran to the girl's bathroom before anyone could see me. I locked the outer door and stood there for a minute without doing anything, hoping no one would need to pee.

Then I just started crying. The tears welled up my eyes and I couldn't stop them. I fell to my knees and sobbed. Suddenly, everything seemed too much—not just gym class and Whitney but everything in school, the cafeteria, the party, Claude, my parents, the video store, everything. I didn't know whom I hated more—myself for being such a dork or Whitney for being such a bitch. I was in there straight through the next period. Several sixth-graders tried to use the bathroom, but I didn't open the door, and I just hoped they wouldn't tell the handyman.

After I had been sitting on the cold bathroom tiles for what seemed like an eternity, I heard a soft knock on the door. "V? Are you in there? V?" I didn't answer. I sniffled into a paper towel and looked at myself in the mirror, red nose and all. I was still wearing my stupid gym uniform.

"V? Let me in. C'mon, it's just me. Sylvia told me you might be in here."

"I'm fine." I laughed hoarsely. "I'm fine, really."

"I know what happened. C'mon."

"Nothing happened. You should go, or you'll be late for

Sister Chandler's class."

"So what?"

"Iz, I'm good, really. I just have stomach problems."

"Can you just open the door? Please?"

I reluctantly opened the door and let her inside.

"You look a mess," she said.

"Is it that bad?"

"*Oui.*" She started wiping my face with a tissue. She zipped open her pink zebra-print handbag and removed a dainty cosmetic case. She began to powder my nose and chin with a fluffy, oversized makeup brush. "There, much better."

"Can I borrow some lipstick?"

"Of course," she said, as she started working on my eyebrows. I closed my eyes, soothed by the gentle motions of her hands on my face. "You should not let them affect you so much," she chided.

"Can we not talk about it?"

"We will attend at that party," she said.

"I don't know." I sighed. "Maybe it's better if we don't."

"Vicenza," she snapped. "*Pourquoi pas?* He invited us! And he owes us after tutoring him."

"You tutored him."

"*La même chose.*"

"You go," I said stubbornly.

"I'm not going without you."

"Bring Veronique and Leslie instead," I said meanly.

She rolled her eyes. "Don't be like that. I promise, we'll have a good time!"

"Okay, I'll go, but you have to promise not to be mad."

"Why?"

"I'm going to the stupid Soirée," I said, holding my breath.

"What? *Avec qui?* Why?"

"My mom set me up with this guy Freddie—he's a family friend's son. She really wants me to go. She thinks I should try to fit in more."

"But you promised!"

"I know. I'm so sorry."

She pretended to look annoyed. "*Bien.* I'll forgive you. But *tu dois être present à la* party on Friday."

"Maybe."

When we finally left the first-floor bathroom, Sylvia told us that she and some other girls in my class had told Headmaster Humphrey what had happened. "Frosh girl found crying in bathroom" was the biggest scandal of the day. Isobel and I bumped into Whitney on our way to Social Justice.

"I'm sorry," Whitney said, rolling her eyes. I knew she had been forced to apologize to me by the dean. Grosvernor faculty was like that: they got involved in every issue, no matter how small. The girls' school I had gone to in Manila was the same. Was there something about the all-estrogen environment that turned administrators into clucking mother hens? At Gros, if the dean had heard you had been drinking at a weekend party with Monty boys, they called your parents to express concern about your "reputation."

"It's okay," I mumbled, hoping my eyes weren't red anymore.

"Maybe we can, um, hang out some time, at, like, Fisherman's Wharf or something," Whitney suggested, a strange smile on her face. Later, I learned that the dean had threatened her with a rare detention unless Whitney tried to make amends by making "weekend social plans" with me as part of her punishment. Her invitation to Fisherman's Wharf was just another dig. It was a tourist trap, and no one cool ever went there (confirmed by the fact that my family thought Fisherman's Wharf was the greatest thing ever).

"Leave her alone," Isobel hissed.

Georgia poked Whitney from behind, Trish shot us a murderous glare, and the three of them walked off with their noses in the air. When they rounded a corner, we could hear them laughing.

"You have to go to the party," Isobel pleaded.

I sighed. A part of me wanted nothing more to do with any

of them. I knew I was just walking into more drama. But Isobel had stood by me, and I wasn't about to let her down. And in any event, I had always wanted to go to one of Claude Caligari's ragers. For once in my life I actually had plans for the weekend!

FROM: queen_vee@aol.com

TO: amparo.dellarosa@info.ph.com

SENT: Thursday, November 19, 6:25 PM

SUBJECT: party prep!

Hi, Peach,

I got your e-mail. Don't worry about us. You know
Dad knows everyone in the Ministry. Hopefully Kuya
Norbert will just get off with a light fine and we'll all be
laughing about it soon. The only thing is that from now
on we can't tape any shows. I'll just IM you who won
American Idol tomorrow so you don't have to wait. School
is good, thanks. I think I might run for class president next
semester! Anyway, Claude's having a huge rager tomorrow
so I have to help him prepare for the par-tay.

XXOOOO,

V

14

"Party" is Not a Verb

THE FIRST ORDER OF business was getting permission. Since my parents could be totally unreasonable sometimes, I knew there was no way I would be able to get out of the house with their consent if they knew I was headed to some guy's unsupervised blowout. And, unfortunately, I'm too uncoordinated to climb out the window. I would have to recruit an unknowing conspirator. One whom my parents would trust in a heartbeat, someone who was practically family and who had already been given the stamp of approval since, after all, he was my date to the until-midnight Soirée. One who could drive.

Freddie Dalugdugan.

I called him on his cell and asked if he wanted to hang out on Friday night at our church's youth band tryouts. I knew he'd say yes because while Freddie might not possess an ounce of athleticism or style, he was also under the mistaken impression he had a great singing voice. Then I told Mom that Freddie and I were going to hang out with the youth group. It would make her feel better to know there would be other kids there. She'd always encouraged me to participate in group activities; I just hadn't had the heart to tell her I wasn't part of any group.

"What time?" Mom asked.

"There's a meeting at the parish hall at seven, and then afterward we're all getting pizza at Round Table."

"Just make sure you're home by eleven."

"Can we make it midnight? You know it takes forever to get pizza from there!"

"Eleven."

"All right," I grumbled.

But I was still excited that she had fallen for it. I immediately dialed Isobel to tell her we had a ride to the party.

"Woo-hoo!" Isobel exclaimed into her cell phone. "And I just found the perfect outfit!" I hoped it didn't involve anything with marabou.

On Friday I was practically flipping out I was so excited. I couldn't wait to leave the cafeteria. I asked Mom if we could close up early again, and she said okay. I barreled her out of the Sears doors.

"I'm so happy you're becoming more involved in church," Mom said as we drove off.

I nodded, too impatient to feel guilty.

Dad had picked up Brittany earlier and was home from work and studying to get his notary public license. His latest get-rich-quick scheme involved collecting the fees to witness important documents. "Five dollars a signature! Imagine that!" he'd told us. "We'll be rich!" One notarized document at a time.

Brittany followed me upstairs to my room.

"What are you doing?" she asked, watching me stuff a make-up bag into my backpack.

"None of your business, butt face."

"I'm telling Mom!"

"If you tell Mom, I'll tell her you're still drinking powdered milk!" I threatened. Brittany had yet to get used to the taste of fresh American milk. "Icky" she called it. My parents were forever trying to get her to change her milk-drinking habits, especially since fresh milk was so much cheaper than powdered (it was the opposite in Manila). And so much better for you, *hello*. I couldn't imagine that I had lived so long on Tang. As far as I was concerned, fresh orange juice and fresh milk were two of the best benefits of living in America.

She stuck her tongue out at me and ran out of the room, slamming the door.

I took a quick shower, brushed and pulled back my hair into a ponytail, and threw on a hooded sweatshirt and jeans.

Freddie arrived promptly at six-thirty, and I could hear him making small talk with Mom in the living room. I rushed down the stairs, watching Mom's face slightly glower at my unladylike movements.

"Slowly! Slowly!" she ordered. "You move like a herd of hippos!"

I took a breath and measured my steps, trying to hide my irritation. "Hi, Freddie."

"Hi, V."

I pecked Mom on the cheek. "Bye."

"Eleven o'clock!" Mom said. "Have fun!"

Freddie kissed her on the cheek good-bye, too. Like I said, he was practically family. Mom watched us from the front porch as we walked to his little Honda. "Hurry up, I want to practice my scales before tryouts," he said as I climbed into the car.

"Oh, don't worry. We're not going to the band auditions."

"We're not?"

"Nope. We're going to Claude Caligari's party! He invited me. But first we have to pick up my friend Isobel. She lives in Saint Francis Woods, near his house. We can hang out there till it's time to go."

Freddie pulled out of the driveway in silence. "Does your mom know?"

"Of course not! What do you think? She'd never let me go."

"I don't know about this," Freddie said, shaking his head.

"C'mon! We won't stay that long! I really want to go. You know what Filipino parents are like! They never let us do *anything.*"

He didn't answer for a while, but he drove the car toward the freeway ramp, in the right direction headed for the city. "All right. But just this once."

"Don't worry. There's another audition for singers next month," I assured him, happy that he was going to play along.

It took us an hour fighting traffic to get to the city from South San Francisco. I gnawed on my fingernails anxiously. I was so giddy I couldn't even sit still. I wondered if I would get a chance to be alone with Claude. Maybe Whitney wouldn't even be there. Maybe it would happen just like in the movies, and he would suddenly realize where I'd been all his life. And we would run to each other from a great distance, with our arms outstretched, calling each other's name.

"CLAUUUUDE!"

"VEEEEEEEEEE!"

Right.

Isobel was in a bathrobe when we arrived at her house. Her parents were away in Cambridge for an academic conference. I wondered briefly why Isobel didn't throw her own parties since her parents were always away and pretty cool about things—she'd told me she'd been allowed to have wine with dinner since she was ten years old.

"*Bonsoir!*" she said, kissing me on both cheeks. "Are you Fred? I'm Isobel!" she said, giving him the double-cheek air-kiss treatment as well. Freddie looked a bit overwhelmed, but it could just have been her perfume.

"Are you wearing that?" she asked, looking critically at my outfit.

"Duh, I brought clothes to change into!" I said, holding up my bag.

"There's digital cable and HBO on demand, and a DVD player," she told Freddie, leading him into the living room. "Make yourself at home."

"Why? What time are we going?" he asked.

"It starts at eight, so I thought we could get there at eight-thirty. We can't get there early—that's so lame!" I told him. I knew all about this stuff from reading teen novels and watching movies like *She's All That*. Plus, we'd need the whole hour to get ready. I was counting on Isobel to give me one of those awesome makeovers, so I could walk into the party dressed in a stunningly gorgeous outfit and Claude would drool all over me and dump Whitney on the spot.

"Is there anything to eat?" Freddie yelled from the couch.

"There's leftover pâté and some cornichons," Isobel said helpfully.

I noticed Freddie hesitate, but I pleaded with my eyes for him to be cool about it. I really wanted everything to go smoothly, and I was so thrilled to actually be out of the house on a Friday night, I was light-headed with the prospect of what was in store. So what if I had to get home by eleven?

Freddie opened the refrigerator door, and Isobel and I disappeared into her bedroom.

I unzipped my backpack and pulled out a red dress with crisscross straps and flouncy hem that I had bought at a deep discount from a store at the mall. "Is it okay?" I asked her.

"*Très* chic! *Parfait!*" she gushed.

"What do you think of mine?" she asked, holding up a hanger that contained an electric fuchsia dress with a deep V-necked halter top and purple snakeskin accents. No marabou, thank God.

I spoke too soon. Just as I was telling her how much I liked her dress, she pulled a fluffy feather boa out of her closet. "I got one for you, too!" she said, handing me its twin. "Aren't they fabulous?"

She threw it over my neck and we looked at our reflections in the mirror. The feathers—both a vibrant, blinding white, had a kooky charm.

We changed into our party clothes and strutted around the

room throwing our feather boas over our shoulders. I let Isobel paint my face with what felt like ten pounds of makeup. I winced as she curled my eyelashes.

"Ouch! Do you have to pull so hard?"

"One must suffer to be beautiful," she said, moving on to my other eye. "Just think of Marilyn Monroe."

I looked at myself in her full-length mirror and smiled. Isobel was better than one of those pushy ladies at the Bloomingdale's cosmetic counter. I barely even recognized myself. I plugged in Isobel's flatiron and we took turns helping each other with our hair.

"Ready?" she asked, smoothing down her spiky hair and putting on her eyeglasses.

"As I'll ever be." I sighed, wondering if this was a good idea. I hated the fact that I'd had to lie to my parents for this to happen, and I had begun to feel guilty about the whole thing. What if something bad happened? What if we got in an accident? What if they found out I was going to a party? I would be in *so* much trouble.

When we left the room, Freddie was comfortably laid out on the couch, chatting on his cell phone and munching on the tiny green pickles. "Yeah, it's the coffee shop on Presidio." He looked up when we entered. Isobel and I struck poses.

"What do you know—still ugly," he said.

"Ignore him," I told Isobel.

"I will." She laughed.

I looked at my watch. It was eight-twenty. Party time.

St. Francis Woods was by far my favorite part of the city. It has the feeling of a secluded, leafy suburb—but it's right in the middle of the metropolis. We drove off Isobel's street to turn to Claude's and found the little cul-de-sac fully clogged with so many cars, I didn't think we would ever find a park-ing spot.

Freddie insisted on driving all the way up to the house to drop us off before he parked, but I wanted to be as inconspicu-ous as possible. "No, let's just park over there," I said, pointing to the next block over.

"There's no space. You guys just get out and I'll meet you inside," he said, zooming up the private driveway. "I've got to make a few calls anyway."

Part of me was glad we wouldn't have to walk in with Freddie, who was wearing an ugly purple rugby shirt and had belted his pleated khaki pants in the middle of his stomach, but another part of me was worried about just the two of us walking in. I suddenly felt we needed strength in numbers.

Isobel shrugged and slicked back her hair. "C'mon, V," she said. I swiveled out of the car, carefully balancing on a borrowed pair of Isobel's spike heels. (Mom never let me wear anything that high.) Isobel joined me and we linked arms and walked up the porch steps. She pressed the doorbell.

"It's open!" someone yelled.

We looked at each other in fright.

I pushed the door open with a tiny shove, and the two of us walked inside. We stood in the middle of an empty hallway decorated with duck prints and a brass umbrella stand. Loud rap music boomed from a back room, so we walked in, fully expecting to find a huge crowd.

But the only person inside was Claude, who was crouched in front of a complicated stereo system. He looked up from the console and turned the volume up a notch. "That's better. Hey, guys. Glad you could make it."

"Pas problème," Isobel said. "We were in the area."

"Yeah, it was like, no big deal . . ."

"There's a bar in the back and food in the kitchen. Help yourselves." He smiled, standing up. He was wearing a blue cashmere sweater that brought out the blue in his eyes. I swooned.

"Um, where is everybody?" I asked. "There are so many cars out front . . ."

"Oh." Claude shrugged. "I think my neighbor's having some kind of black-tie shindig. Actually, you guys are the first to arrive."

I felt my stomach sink.

"Claude, there's no ice!" We heard a familiar voice complain from the foyer.

Whitney walked in carrying two cocktail glasses. She was wearing a pair of faded cargo pants, a simple tank top and flip-flops. I suddenly felt ridiculous in my three-inch heels and white feather boa. She smirked. "What is it, Mardi Gras or something? You two look like a drag show.

"Here," she said, handing Claude his drink and deliberately turning away from us.

Isobel and I moved to the kitchen to strategize. It was agonizing being the only two people at the party aside from the host and his girlfriend. Our whole casual "drop-by" lost all its insouciance.

"Drink?" Isobel asked, appraising the stocked bar.

I shook my head. "I'm too nervous," I said, not wanting to admit that I'd never taken a drink in my life. I didn't want to make a fool of myself any more than I already was.

"There's no wine or champagne," she said grumpily. "And I hate beer."

She poured us both a tall glass of ice water. We tiptoed out to the garden to look at the landscaping around the kidney-shaped pool, which boasted an adjoining Jacuzzi.

"Well, we're here," I said, looking around helplessly. I had never been to a party. I didn't know what to do.

"Oui," Isobel said disconsolately. I think she had been hoping we would blend in with the crowd. But, unfortunately, we had arrived too early for that. I think her French ego was bruised by our faux pas. We sat by the pool for a few minutes, sipping our water and watching the steam rise from the hot tub. Suddenly, the pleasant atmosphere was broken by a braying yodel.

"PAARRRTAYYYY!!!!"

We looked up to see one of Claude's lacrosse teammates wearing a Burger King crown askew on his head. He was hoisting a case of beer in his arms. Following him were all the coolest people from Monty and Gros.

The party had finally begun.

You know how, in movies, parties are always filled with what looks like hundreds and hundreds of people (otherwise known as extras)? And everyone is dancing crazily and grinding in three-person lambada (the "forbidden" dance) sandwiches and hitting on each other? Well, this party was nothing like that. I didn't know what to expect—maybe I'd seen too many *American Pie* movies and MTV *Spring Break* specials. I mean, I guess it was fun and all, but it was also—I don't know, just not what I expected. There couldn't have been more than forty people there. Mostly it was just a bunch of people sitting around, drinking. For hours, Isobel and I flitted around aimlessly watching some Monty and Gros juniors flip quarters into shot glasses. One girl devised a drinking game wherein each person had to see who could hold a beer cap between their butt cheeks the longest, which was more entertaining than it sounds. And we had totally lost track of Freddie, whom we didn't see all evening once he dropped us off.

Isobel and I were sitting by the side near the Jacuzzi watching people push each other into the pool (finally some action!) when I looked at my watch and couldn't believe it was already a few minutes past eleven. Time flies when you're watching Georgia Wilson pinch a Heineken bottle cap between her butt cheeks.

"I have to get home!" I told her. "You find Freddie, I just need to use the bathroom. Where do you think it is?"

I was a little worried about breaking my first-ever curfew, then remembered I was with Freddie, whom my parents utterly worshipped. I asked a couple of girls who were funneling beers in the kitchen where the bathroom was and they pointed upward. "Third door on the right. The ones on the first floor are all being used." One of them cackled knowingly.

I had to fight through the entire Monty lacrosse team to get upstairs. Claude's house was gargantuan. I was a little intimidated about being on the second floor, which was quiet and empty.

Following the girls' directions, I tapped on the third door and tried the knob. "Is anyone there?" I asked. It was open, so I walked in. I closed the door behind me, making certain the door was locked. Then I heard a strange noise emanating from behind the shower curtain. I pulled it back.

"Claude!"

He was slumped into the bathtub, legs dangling over the side. "Ehhh?" he asked, opening one eye. I had to admit, even in that state, he was still really cute.

"What are you doing here?" I asked, then felt foolish. It was his house—he could pass out anywhere he felt like.

"Hey, it's V. Hi, Veeeeee," he said, grinning.

"Hi," I said, sitting on the edge of the tub. I'd hardly seen him the whole evening after Isobel and I arrived. He and Whitney disappeared for a while, then he was busy circulating. It was too hard to capture his attention.

I was kind of thrilled to finally be alone with him, even if he was barely conscious and smelled like a keg.

"Are you having fun?" he drawled.

"Yeah, yeah, it's a great party," I told him, even if I'd been pretty bored the whole time.

"That's great—that's what I like to hear." He sighed, nodding vigorously. His head snapped back suddenly and hit the faucet. "Ow! That hurt!"

"Ooops!" I said, and almost laughed. "Here, let me help," I said, pulling his hand.

"Yeah, I should probably try to get out of here," he said. "Good idea."

I put an arm around his waist and felt his hot breath on my cheek. I'd dreamed about this moment many times, but never like this.

He leaned on my shoulder and rested his head in the crook of my neck. I led him to the door, but when I tried to open it, I found I had locked us in when I was being ultravigilant about privacy. The doorknob wouldn't budge.

"Shit!" I said, rattling the door. "It's stuck!" I told Claude.

"Thuck?" he repeated. "How can it be thuck?" He began to hiccup.

I began to pound on it. "Help! Help! Anyone! The door's stuck!"

No one answered. *My cell phone!* I thought. I'll just call Isobel. I fumbled in my bag to get it, but couldn't find it. I must have left it at Isobel's when I dumped out my makeover supplies. I was so impatient to get ready for the party, I hadn't even noticed I'd left without it.

Claude crumpled against me, and I helped him sit on the closed toilet. He couldn't hold himself upright, and he slid to the floor and dropped his head against the porcelain. Okay. Not a great visual. But, believe me, he was still cute.

"Vicenza . . . I need you . . ." he gurgled.

"Yes?" My heart began to beat faster.

"To hand me that wastebasket."

I pushed it over to his side and he retched violently into it.

Ew.

When he threw up again, I felt guilty enough to try to hold his head up so he wouldn't puke on himself. Kind of gross, but I felt bad for the guy.

The minutes ticked by. A couple of times, I got up and rapped on the door and bellowed, but the party was so loud no one heard me.

"I'm hot!" he suddenly announced. "God, I'm really hot! Isn't it really hot in here!—" *hic* "Hey! I gotta—" *hic* "—take my clothes off!" He began to unbutton his shirt, bellowing that Nelly song.

"Uh—Claude—I don't know if that's such a . . ." I said, but it was too late. Somehow he'd found the energy to strip off his shirt and jeans, and had hopped back in the bathtub wearing nothing but his boxer shorts.

He reeled from side to side, fumbled with the faucet, and sent a blast of water from the shower head, with the curtain open. It was the kind of nozzle that you could take off the hook and spritz your body with, and he began to do just that, except he was spritzing water everywhere. The mirror. The sink. The Japanese prints on the wall.

I was suddenly anxious that he might cause some real damage or else slip, hit his head, and pass out.

"Turn it off! Turn it off!" I said, scrambling to switch off the water.

"Hee-hee, hee-hee," he snickered, like a little boy. "This is fun!"

Just then, I heard Isobel's voice from the hallway. "VICENZA??? ARE YOU IN THERE???"

"VICENZA, what's going on?" That was Freddie.

"IZ! FREDDIE! HELP! I'M LOCKED IN!!!" I yelled, laughing, as Claude and I fought over the shower controls. "Stop it! You're going to make me wet, too! Stop!" I grabbed the shower head away from him and mercifully switched off the water.

"What's going on?" Isobel asked.

"The door—it's locked somehow. We can't get it open!" I yelled.

"We?"

I heard Freddie and Isobel arguing about the best course of action. Isobel wanted to kick down the door, but Freddie wanted to try and open it with a credit card. They finally stopped bickering and managed to jigger the door open from the other side. They burst in, just as Claude wrestled the shower head away from me, and we both fell backward in the tub.

"*Mon dieu!*" Isobel exclaimed. We must have looked a sight—

Claude in his boxers, me utterly drenched.

"What's going on?" Freddie asked, looking confused.

"Let go!" I told Claude, grabbing the shower head away from his hand.

"Nooo!" he screamed, taking it back.

"What the hell is going on?"

We both looked up and saw Whitney standing at the doorway between Freddie and Isobel.

Boy, did she not look happy.

Behind her was a crowd gathered in front of the bathroom because of all the commotion. Whitney's face was so red, I could have sworn steam was pouring out of her nostrils. I'd never seen her so angry. Whitney was the queen of cool. She never lost her composure.

I grabbed the shower head and pushed Claude off me.

"Give it back, give it back!" he whined, meaning his new toy. Oh well. It was his house. I dropped it in the tub, and he picked it up with a happy smile on his face.

"Have you been in there with him the whole time?" Whitney demanded.

"Me? Yeah—we were locked in," I explained, as Isobel helped me to my feet. I dripped fat wet drops on the tile. So much for my dry-clean-only dress. "It was an accident," I told her, as Freddie handed me a towel.

"You don't say," she snapped.

"What's your problem?" I asked her, still finding a lot of humor in the situation.

"The whole time? It was just the two of you?"

I didn't even know what she was getting at. "Yeah, but it was all a mistake."

"Don't you EVER come near him again!" she screeched.

"Whatever," I said, backing off.

She shoved her way past me and glared at Claude, who was sitting in a couple of inches of water, fumbling with the shower nozzle. "Get up! Get up! And for God's sake, put some clothes on!" she barked.

Freddie and Isobel were still staring at me.

"Can we go?" I said. "It's way past my curfew, and I am so dead. But first, I really have to find another bathroom."

We closed the door behind us, just in time to hear Whitney scream.

Claude had just found the shower's on switch again.

On the car ride home, everyone was silent. "We couldn't find you for the longest time," Isobel said. "We looked for you everywhere. And you did not answer your cell."

"I didn't have it on me," I explained. "I think I might have left it at your house."

"Yeah, we were really worried," Freddie agreed. "So what did happen in there?"

"I told you guys. I was locked in! By accident!"

"Are you sure that's all that happened?" Isobel asked.

"Of course! What do you mean?"

Freddie shrugged. It was only then I noticed that there was someone else in the car with us. "Hey, I'm V," I said.

"I'm Tess," she said. She was the girl in Freddie's beauty pageant picture. *"Kamusta na?"*

I said I was okay. I looked at my watch. It was past midnight! My parents would think I was dead or, worse, kidnapped.

FROM: queen_vee@aol.com

TO: amparo.dellarosa@info.ph.com

SENT: Friday, November 20, 1:30 AM

SUBJECT: awesome party!

So, I just got back from Claude's total kick-ass bash! I'm still soooo tired. It was a major rager with tons of people. Super fun! His house was like, gi-normous. I couldn't even find the bathroom! Seriously, you wouldn't believe it—people were like cannonballing off the roof into the pool and the police came to break it up, just like in the movies! But during the whole thing, Claude never left my side. He was so attentive, we spent most of the party together. It was SO romantic, he told me how much he needed me, and I held his head in my lap and everything.

Love,

V

15
Diane Sawyer Is Always Right

I WALKED IN THE door, fully expecting my parents to chew my ears off. Instead, the two of them were sitting on the couch with silly grins on their faces.

"Hey, what's up?" I said, hoping I had wiped off all traces of lipstick and mascara at Isobel's, where I had changed out of my party clothes.

"Vicenza!" Mom smiled. She stood up and gave me a hug.

"I'm sorry I'm so late."

"It's okay."

"It is?"

"Didn't you get any of our messages?" Dad asked.

"No . . . um, and I would have called but I didn't have my cell on me. Freddie's car stalled on the freeway. He called Triple-A but no one came for hours. . . ." I babbled. Freddie and I had agreed we would both blame car troubles for missing curfew.

"We know. Tita Connie called and told us," she said. Good old Freddie.

"So you weren't worried?" I asked suspiciously.

"No, no. Freddie's a good boy."

This was so unlike my parents. Even with Freddie involved, I couldn't believe how mellow they were acting. Where was the lecture? The yelling? My parents had sat me down for five hours when I came home from the mall with a second piercing in my left ear. Dad had threatened to cut off my allowance forever, and Mom had said she had never been so disappointed. They both questioned what kind of evil influence "America was exerting on our daughter." Just because I had gotten a second hole in my ear! It was a moot point since it got infected and I had to take the earring out. And here I was, walking in after my curfew the first time I had ever been out on a Friday night and they were cool with it? What was going on? Had they been replaced by aliens?

Mom was beet red and couldn't stop laughing. Dad was practically beaming. The two of them were acting seriously strange.

"Mom, are you drunk?" I asked.

"A little . . . a little. Daddy made some margaritas." Mom giggled.

"What's going on?" I demanded. My parents never drank. Mom was practically allergic—every time she had a sip of wine her face turned purple.

"Should we tell her?" Dad asked.

"Why not? She'll find out soon enough." Mom laughed.

"What?"

The two of them turned.

"WE WON THE LOTTERY!!"

"WHAT?"

"We won! Look, look!" Mom said, waving a piece of paper in the air. "We found it in the mailbox when Daddy finally got it open!"

"We did?" I didn't know what to think. I was seized by wild, irrational joy mingled with anxiety. Had we really won? Or were my parents simply out of their minds? It seemed too good to be true. But then Dad was so firm in his belief that one day things would work out for us, I was tempted to believe him. Why would my parents play such a cruel joke on me like this? My heart began to flutter wildly. Were all our problems with money truly over?

Dad began shouting. "I *told* you! I *told* you!"

"Dad's numbers went through? Did we really win?" I asked, my voice squeaking. Oh my God. Oh my God. Oh my God. I couldn't breathe. We won LOTTO??? This was crazy.

"No! No! The numbers, no! But, yes! We won! Here, look!" Mom thrust an envelope in my hand.

"'You may be a winner!'" I read aloud, my fingers shaking. It was a letter from the Publishers Clearing House, saying Mr. Jose Rizal Arambullo may have already won the grand prize of twenty-five million dollars in the annual sweepstakes. It almost made sense, since Dad certainly subscribed to a lot of their magazines. But as I continued to read the fine print, I began to realize my parents had made a *colossal* mistake. A disgustingly stupid, pathetic, moronic, absurd, only-an-immigrant-could-make-it mistake.

"We didn't win," I said flatly, folding the paper.

"What do you mean? It says we're the top finalists! And that we may have already won," Mom said, her voice quavering.

"It says you *may* be a winner. It's not quite the same as actually *being* the winner. And, anyway, if Dad had won, there'd be, like, a camera crew and Ed McMahon here. Where's Ed McMahon, Mom? It's just a scam, I can't believe you guys fell for it. Diane Sawyer did a story on it on *Primetime* the other night." Diane Sawyer had done a total exposé of it, and if they didn't believe me, I knew they would believe Diane Sawyer.

"Are you sure?" Mom asked.

"*Hindi tayo nanalo?*" Dad asked. "*Bakit?*" (We didn't win?! Why?)

I explained to them how these companies worked, sending false, misleading information to bolster sales of their products. "It's totally bogus, Dad."

"Bow-gus? What does that mean? Stop talking slang!" Mom said angrily.

"It means it's bunk, it's a fraud, it's a lie. There's no twenty-five-million-dollar bounty waiting for us at the end of the rainbow!" I was quickly forgetting my relief at not being grounded for life and was becoming increasingly annoyed at how naïve my parents were acting. Wasn't I supposed to be the kid here?

"It's not true? The letter? But it's on official stationery. There's even a seal on it!" Dad said indignantly.

"Why would they lie? Why would anyone do that? It says we may have already won. All we need to do is send out for more magazines and we can claim our prize," Mom argued.

"I'm telling you, Mom. Diane Sawyer said it's a scam."

"Diane said? Are you sure? Diane really said that?"

"Positive."

My parents looked at me doubtfully, but Diane Sawyer's word was unimpeachable in our house. They idolized her. She was their only source of news, next to Regis Philbin, Katie Couric, Barbara Walters, Meredith Vieira, and all the rest of the women on *The View*.

When the truth sank in, they began to get angry. "They shouldn't be allowed to send letters like this! That's a crime!" Dad said.

"Imagine that, telling people they might have won the sweep-stakes!"

"We should sue!"

"*Buti nalang* we didn't tell anyone yet. Imagine how embarrassing that would have been! Thank God we waited for you!"

"*Mga tarantado!*" (What wickedness!)

Dad tore up the letter in a million little pieces in fury. "That's what I think of that!" Then he looked at his watch. "Ayayay, it's one in the morning!"

"What are you doing home so late anyway?" Mom asked, suddenly focusing on the fact that I had broken my first-ever curfew.

I should have kept my mouth shut.

It took the better part of the weekend to cheer my parents up from the depression that not winning twenty-five-million dollars had wrought. I could overhear them talking in the kitchen while I did my homework. Things were looking bad. Cousin Norbert was under investigation, so the tape-smuggling business was still on hold, and my dad still hadn't had any luck convincing the other Sears stores in the area to let us open up an Arambullo Food Services in their employees' cafeterias. Dad's import-export business was bringing in zero, and Mom had stopped selling homemade longanisas after Tita Connie and Tito Ebet asked for a "sales commission." The "commission" from selling the sausages to their friends practically wiped out any profit my parents could derive from the business. Meanwhile, rent was due and the tuition bills were looming.

On Saturday, Mom didn't even come to the cafeteria with me. She had fallen ill with a cold, possibly from all the excitement. Dad had to drive me to Sears, and on the way there, he was philosophical about the entire thing.

"You know, V, the thing is, we didn't really think we had won," he said, one hand on the steering wheel and the other draped over the open window.

Dad was weaving in and out of traffic, cutting people off, and turning left and right without signaling. It had taken him three tries to get his driver's license. Dad complained that Americans followed "too many rules." In the Philippines, such things as traffic signals and turning lanes were nonissues. On the off chance that Dad was caught by the police, he would slip them a five-hundred-peso bill with his driver's license. But Dad already had two points on his American license; he couldn't afford another speeding ticket.

"Careful, Dad, you almost hit that post," I said, gripping the armrest of my seat tightly. I had never noticed how badly Dad drove back home, since everyone else drove the same way. I decided I preferred the American way, especially when the van suddenly racked up and down on speed bumps, which Dad drove over blithely without slowing down.

"But there's no saying that we didn't win, either," he said. "I sent the thing away."

"You ordered another magazine, Dad?" I groaned.

"*US Weekly*. I don't give up," he said cheerfully. "Mark my words, one day, we will win. It's just a matter of time."

"If you say so."

"So, how were the tryouts?"

"All right," I hedged. "It's really competitive. I don't know if we made it. Think Mom's going to be okay?" I asked, changing the subject. I still couldn't believe I'd gotten off so easily.

"Oh yeah. She'll be fine," Dad said, whistling. "It's just a cold."

Dad drove into the Costco lot. We had to pick up a week's supply of food and paper goods for the cafeteria. Plus, Dad and I loved visiting Costco for the free food samples.

"Look! Little hot dogs—let's get some," he said, just as we had stacked several bags of frozen chicken breasts on our cart.

We munched our way through the special salsa, the fish crackers, the ginger mayonnaise, and the mini pizzas.

"No need to get breakfast!" Dad said.

The flat loading cart was stacked with towers of paper plates, Dixie cups, and napkins. We had several huge slabs of cold cuts, from ham to turkey breast. We began to unload on the rolling counter at the checkout. "Could you make sure not to tax us on the paper goods?" Dad asked. "They're for resale."

The clerk nodded and resumed punching numbers. The total flashed as small red letters on the cash register: $334.40. Dad wrote a check and handed it to the clerk. She punched in several numbers and waited. "I'm sorry, sir. We can't accept your check," she said.

"What?" Dad asked, a hand on his wallet. "Why?"

"Sorry, sir, it says check unacceptable. Do you have a credit card? Or there's an ATM machine over there," the clerk said.

I stood behind Dad. "What's going on? Is everything okay?"

Dad took the check back nervously. "No, no. Let's go."

"Let's go?" I asked dumbly. I didn't understand.

"I said let's go," Dad said in an irritated voice.

I followed him out to the parking lot. It had taken us a good hour to shop for the supplies. We climbed into the van. "They wouldn't take my check," Dad said, almost to himself.

I was scared. I couldn't understand what just happened. Had we run out of money? What was going on? And what were we going to do? We were low on nacho chips and turkey breast, paper plates, and Kit Kat bars. How would I run the cafeteria without them?

"Is everything okay?" I asked. I suddenly understood the desperate hopefulness my parents had showed last night. Things really were bad since the video store was raided. I tried not to think about it.

"It's okay," Dad said. "We should have cash by tomorrow—we'll do the shopping then," he assured me, but I sensed a note of doubt in his voice.

Dad dropped me off at Sears. I set up everything like I always did, and wished Mom were around to help me with the sandwiches. It was difficult having to run the register, sling drinks, and put together orders all by myself, and trying to explain why we didn't have certain things on the menu was making me edgy. At the end of the day, I was practically wiped out from exhaustion. I sat on the table behind the counter and stretched my legs. My foot hit something small and metallic.

I looked underneath the table. It was my missing cell phone. It must have fallen out of my backpack yesterday afternoon even before I got to Isobel's.

I pocketed it and looked up to see the doors swinging open, happy to see a friendly face underneath a bright red baseball cap. But instead of coming up to the counter for his Pepsi, Paul just walked straight to the back. I heard him drop coins into the machine and the whirr-flop of the soda can as it fell to the bottom. I heard the door slam as he exited through the back door.

Ooookay. That was strange. What was going on? Not even saying hello and then totally ignoring me. I pulled out my cell phone to complain to Isobel, and I noticed the message light was blinking.

"You have four new messages," the electronic machine voice said. "First message, Friday, 7:15 P.M. To play, press one." I pressed the button.

A guy's deep voice.

I dropped the phone. Oh my God.

Last night was *Friday.*

The Stephen King movie!

Paul!

I ran out the door after him. He was drinking his Pepsi by the open stacks of products, near the Craftsman drills and tool sets. "Hey!" I said.

"Oh, it's you," he said, turning away.

"Paul, please, I'm so sorry about last night. It just slipped my mind. I am so lame. I'm so sorry."

He shrugged. "It's cool."

"It's totally a big deal for me. I'm so embarrassed. I hope you didn't have to wait too long."

"Really, it's no big deal."

"Look, things are really weird right now . . . my family is like, falling apart. . . . My Dad's check was rejected at Costco. . . . Last night they thought they won the lottery," I began to ramble incoherently. "I'm just so out of it. . . ."

"Look, don't even worry about it," he said.

"Okay." I shrugged. There was a long, awkward silence. I felt so bad. I couldn't believe I had completely forgotten about it.

"Hey, are you done with those books I lent you?" he asked abruptly.

I nodded. They were in my backpack at the cafeteria.

"Cool. When you get a chance, can I have them back?"

"Sure."

"Great. Well, see ya," he said.

"Bye."

I closed up shop in, like, five minutes flat. I felt a ball of hurt and disappointment clench my stomach. I hadn't meant to hurt his feelings. I thought about how he must have waited at the theater, all alone. God, I knew what that felt like. But still, it wasn't like a date or anything. We were just friends. At least, we used to be friends. I was so angry at myself I slammed the pantry door just as my cell phone rang.

"What?" I said sullenly.

"Is that any way to answer the phone?" Dad asked.

"Sorry."

"Can you take the bus home?" Dad asked. He explained he

was still too busy studying for his notary exam at the library to pick me up.

"Fine!" I said, annoyed that on top of everything, I had a long forty-five-minute bus ride to look forward to. We only lived fifteen minutes from the mall, but the SamTrans bus took such a long way around, it was almost a scenic route. I stuffed the red tin can with the day's take ($80, half what a week of supplies cost at Costco), jammed it into my backpack, turned off the lights, dropped Paul's books by his employee locker, and stormed out of Sears.

Ugh. I *hated* Sears!

The Gros girls were right. It was the tackiest store in the universe.

In Manila, my family would never even shop at a store like Sears. In Manila, I would never have this kind of problem. First of all, in Manila, I was *popular*. That's what sucked so much about living in America. Just when it mattered the most, all the rules had changed, and I was suddenly out of the game.

An hour later, I finally walked up our driveway. "Mom, I'm home!" I yelled from the front door. I was still depressed about Paul and headachy from the bus ride. I didn't want to do anything but hole myself up in my room and turn up the new Blink-182 album. Mom was sitting on the couch wrapped in a blanket, with a paper in her lap.

"What's up?" I asked.

She held up the page, and with growing horror, I realized it was a printout of an e-mail to Peaches.

"Do you want to explain yourself?" she asked.

16
Joining the Joy-Luck Club

I'VE BEEN GROUNDED indefinitely. I'll probably rot in my room until eternity. Which is fine, because I'm not sure I really want to leave it anyway. Maybe there's a chance for home-schooling yet.

Mom is F-U-R-I-O-U-S. But I can't tell who's angrier: Mom, because I lied to her, or me, because she invaded my privacy. Wasn't I entitled to my own cyberspace? Even just a little bit? Where did she get off reading other people's personal thoughts. When I grow up and have children, I will never treat them this way, I vowed.

"How'd you get that?" I asked, when I recognized what she was holding in her hand.

"You hate your Soirée dress?" Mom asked. "The one we bought at the outlet?"

"No, Mom, I don't. I swear. Give me that, *please*, it's *mine.* . . ."

She read aloud: "'It's got a butt bow. . . .'"

"Why'd you go through my account?"

"You left it on the screen. I went to close it, but then I saw this and I just started reading it." She shrugged her shoulders helplessly. Thank God Mom didn't open the other e-mails. God knows what she would think of all the lies I'd fed my best friend. She would probably think I was crazy. Maybe I am.

"It's not true."

"What's not true?"

"What's in there. I like the dress, Mom, I promise."

"No, you're lying to me. Stop lying to me!"

"I'm not lying."

"You are! Just admit you hate it!"

"I don't hate it!"

"It's right here. You say you hate it! Why can't you just be honest with me for once?" Mom asked.

"I don't hate it! You're getting it all wrong! That wasn't for you to read! Mom, can you please give it back?"

"You said it was ugly!"

"It's not ugly! It's great, Mom, please!"

"What am I supposed to believe?" she asked.

"Believe me!"

"Why? You lie to me! You lie!" With that, the worst thing of all happened. Mom started to cry.

"Don't cry, Mom. I'm a horrible person. It's not true what I wrote," I pleaded. "Please, Mommy, you've got to believe me. Please don't cry."

Mom sniffed into a tissue and blew her nose. "I don't know. I don't know. So hurtful. So hurtful. Hits here," she said, patting her chest.

"What's going on? Why are you fighting?" Brittany asked, appearing in the doorway with a Popsicle.

"Nothing," I said.

"Brittany, go to your room, *iha*."

"Why are you crying, Mom?"

"I said GO TO YOUR ROOM!" Mom roared.

Brittany disappeared, dripping Popsicle juice on the floor.

Mom was muttering to herself. "You know, you're entitled to your own opinion. You just should have told me you didn't like it. What a waste of money! Do you know how hard Daddy and I work so you can go to that school? And all you say is that you hate it, that everyone will make fun of you, and that they'll laugh when they see you."

"Mom, stop, please stop. Please."

She began to weep uncontrollably. "Daddy and I are doing our best. We didn't want to leave Manila. But we had to, we had to." She rummaged in the box for another tissue. "We didn't have a choice. We had to move to America. But if we had known this was going to happen! Our children talking back to us. Our children so miserable. So miserable! That's what you said, right? That you're miserable! You don't even know!" she raged.

"Don't know what? Why we had to move?" She was right, I didn't know.

"Daddy's partner, Ponce Sorriano, in the bank. Embezzled all the money. All the money. We were bankrupt. Daddy's best friend! Stole all the money! Fled! And left Daddy with nothing! And everyone said Daddy should sue, but Daddy didn't. We decided to come to America for a new start. We could have moved to the province. Daddy's family still has onion plantations in Nueva Ecija, but where would that leave you and Brittany? We wanted better for you girls. Better life! Some life this is! Some life!"

I sat on the couch, paralyzed. I didn't know. I had a suspicion that our moving had to do with something bad that had happened with Dad's business. But my parents had always been so cheerful about everything. They never even talked about it— never ever brought up *why* we had to leave.

"The province—you guys were thinking of moving to the province?" I asked, inwardly cringing. Nobody lived in the province. I couldn't even imagine it. Mom's family had always been from Manila, but I knew Dad's family came from some big province up north. But I didn't think he would ever want to go back there. Moving from Manila to Nueva Ecija was like moving from New York to Omaha, but even worse. They didn't have malls or cable TV or Starbucks in Nueva Ecija!

"Cheaper! We couldn't afford the maids, the house, the car, the guards anymore. Daddy and I thought about it. We said we had to downsize. To live a little more simply! But then we said, no, we'll go to America! So we're here! For you! For you and Brittany! Only for you! And then we move here, only to find out that the rumor in Manila is that Daddy embezzled money, too! Your dad! Can you imagine? They think we're so rich because we send you to Grosvernor School!"

"What, who says?"

"Everybody in Manila! Can you imagine our humiliation! But, no, we don't say anything! Let them gossip! Let them talk!" Mom said bitterly.

"I don't understand. . . ."

"Everyone's saying how can the Arambullos say they are bankrupt when the girls go to the best private school in San Francisco! Daddy must have taken money, too! Daddy must have let the bank fail! Daddy must have been in on it! So many lies! Lies! You know how Filipinos are! They can't wait to kick you when you're down! And all Daddy and I have is how proud we are of the two of you! Everything for you! And this is how you thank us!"

"I never asked you to move!" I screamed. "You didn't even ask me what I wanted! Did you think I wanted to come here?

Away from all my friends? Do you even realize I practically don't have any friends here? You don't know anything about my life, Mom! I work after school and on Saturdays and I still try to keep up a three point eight GPA! Do you think I wanted this for myself? Did you? Did you?"

We were getting as ridiculous as one of those tawdry Filipino soap operas my grandmother and I were addicted to—the shows where dewy-eyed actresses in the starring roles played much-abused orphans.

Mom and I gaped at each other in shock. We had never spoken to each other this way. Mom didn't have the easiest childhood. Actually, it was something out of an Amy Tan novel. Her dad was old-school Chinese, with the goatee and the Fu Manchu mustache. I was always a little scared of Grandfather, even if by the time I was born, he had mellowed out and was a fat, quiet old man. Mom told me how Grandfather's family had disinherited him after he married my grandmother, who was half Norwegian and a Catholic. Mom's greatest wish was to have the kind of loving, stable family that wouldn't yell and scream like we were doing now.

She threw the paper to the floor. "I always thought, I always thought—that we had a special connection, you and I," Mom said. "I know you and Daddy are close, but I thought we had a nice relationship, too. I don't trust you anymore. You were my girl. But you have broken my heart. You have ruined it. Ruined every-thing."

"I'm sorry, Mom," I whispered. "I'm just so, so sorry." She left the room, and I knelt down to pick up my correspondence.

Mom and I had fought before, but never like this. We just didn't seem to be able to talk to each other anymore. I didn't know what was going on. I wish we had never come here. I wish we had never moved to America. If we had never moved to America, Mom and I wouldn't have fought like this. I wouldn't have to make up stories about my pathetic life to my best friend because I would actually have one. I was too shocked and angry and confused and sad to cry.

I never knew Tito Ponce had betrayed my father. I didn't know that was why we had to leave. I didn't know my parents had even considered moving to the province. It was too much information. I was only fourteen. I didn't need to know *everything*. I went online and deleted all the e-mails I had sent Peaches.

Later, Mom knocked on the door to my room.

"Come in," I said meekly.

She walked in, and her eyes were still red and puffy. "You're grounded for missing curfew. Freddie told his mom every-thing—because she was so mad he didn't get chosen for the church band she complained to the priest. Father Al told her he never even showed up! So you can forget about going to the Soirée. But I guess that's fine since you hate the dress you were going to wear anyway," Mom said bitterly.

I shrugged. "I'm sorry about the party. I didn't think you would let me go."

"Always no trust! You think Daddy and I are like from medieval times. Why not ask? Why not find a way we can help? No, you lie. Instead, you lie, always you lie."

I looked down at the floor. "I'm sorry."

"And no computer either." She unplugged the laptop and picked it up. "Where is your cell phone?"

I handed it to her, placing it on top of the computer.

When Dad finally came home, Brittany, Mom, and I were seated around a gloomy dinner table.

"What happened? Who died?" Dad asked.

"I'll tell you later," Mom said sharply.

I spent a dismal night in my room, trying to stop thinking about everything. I'd disappointed Paul. I'd disappointed Mom. And when Dad found out what I'd done, he'd be disappointed, too. I didn't even have the energy to worry about e-mailing Peaches. I had absolutely nothing to say.

YOU HAVE NO NEW MESSAGES.

INBOX:

NEW MAIL: 0

SAVED MAIL: 0

DELETED MAIL: 75

17

The Wrong Kind of Popularity Contest

ON MONDAY, DAD dropped us off at school after hardly saying a word to me and Brittany during the hour-long commute. No fun stories of his childhood. No crazy and fantastical conversations about what we would do when we finally won the lottery.

"Bye, Dad," I said tentatively.

He grunted as I closed the door. Brittany headed to the kindergarten room, and I walked up the steps where Isobel was waiting. She ran over when she saw me.

"What happened to you?" she asked. "I called your house and your mom said you cannot take my calls, then I tried your cell and there was no answer. Didn't you get my messages?"

"Long story," I said.

"So you don't know?" she asked, her eyes wide.

"Know what?"

"Incroyable!"

"Know what?" I insisted.

"It's all online." She shook her head.

"Online? What are you talking about?"

She looked at her watch. "Okay, we have a little time before first period. Let's go to the computer lab. I'll show you."

Several girls from our class looked at me when we arrived at the lab. "Wow. It's always the quiet ones, you know," one snickered.

"Congratulations," another remarked. "Look who's here, Vicenza, the numero uno herself!"

I didn't even know they knew who I was. I was so used to being invisible. Apart from Isobel, no one ever said hi to me in the hallways.

Isobel logged onto the web. "Here," she said, showing me the web page she had called up on the screen.

"Oh my God!"

"I know."

"Why am I there? What did I do?"

"Is it true?" Sylvia Abernofsky asked, coming over and leaning over the chair. "Whitney said that you totally stole her boyfriend and made out with him in the bathroom for three hours!" Her voice lowered, scandalized. "She said you guys even *showered* together!"

"Is that what she's saying?" I asked.

"It's what everyone's saying. It's even on this site," she said, opening another browser window and pointing to a "sighting" on Claude's fan site. "You were at the rager on Friday night at Claude Caligari's?" she asked, a hint of envy in her voice.

"Yeah." I nodded.

"So what happened?" someone asked.

"Tell us! Did the police really get called and break up the party?"

"What's Claude's house like?"

"Oh my God, did you kiss him?"

"In the bathroom?"

"Tell us!"

I sighed and told them the truth: that I was locked in the bathroom with Claude Caligari but nothing happened. I thought about telling them about how he threw up the whole time but decided to be discreet on that point.

"Really, nothing happened. He was passed out in the tub. I was trying to get the door open. That's it. For a whole hour. I thought I'd die because I couldn't pee with him there."

But somehow, I didn't think anyone believed me.

When I walked into Honors English, everyone was sitting around the table chatting. They stopped when they saw me.

"Hi, Vicenza," Carter O'Riordan said. She was a red-haired girl who headed the second-most-popular clique in the freshman class next to Whitney's. I didn't even think she knew my name.

"Did you have a nice weekend?" she asked.

The whole class burst into laughter.

It suddenly occurred to me that I was finally popular. But not in a way I had ever wanted to be.

All that week and the next, I could hardly concentrate, at school or at home. At Gros, everyone was talking about me. They seemed to know not only my name (and how to pronounce it) but also exactly what happened that night (except for the part about me and Claude hooking up, which SO didn't happen), where I lived—everything. Whitney made my life harder and harder. She never passed up a chance to mock or criticize me.

"Who in their right mind would ever wear *brown* stockings?" I heard Whitney ask during ethics class.

My ears burned. Mom had bought me nude-color silk stockings from Hong Kong. They were a valued luxury in Manila. I wasn't really thinking when I put them on that morning—I just reached for the nearest pair that wasn't black, since I was so sick of wearing black tights with my uniform. Apparently, I had committed yet another horrible fashion faux pas.

"I think they are adorable," Isobel said supportively.

"Whatever. I'll take them off later," I said. I was late for the geometry semester final. I was desperately praying I would pass, or else there would be hell to pay when I lost my scholarship.

Claude had arrived uncharacteristically early for the final, and had spent almost the entire time bent over his paper in concentration. Usually, he gave up halfway through and turned in an incomplete sheet. When he turned in his test this time, I noticed it was black with eraser markings and crossed-out answers.

"How'd you do?" I asked, after I'd handed my exam in.

"All right." He grinned. "I think I actually did all right for once."

"That's great."

"By the way, V, I'm sorry about the other night. I was *so* wasted."

"Yeah, it's no big deal," I said. As I said it I realized, it really wasn't. When I looked at Claude, my heart didn't go pitter-patter anymore. He was just a guy. Just a guy. Just a slightly dim, kind of goofy jock. That was all. He wasn't deep or smart or funny or in any way interesting. He was blond and had blue eyes, and he didn't even look one iota like Tobey. In fact, what was I thinking? He looked . . . well, rather ordinary, come to think about it.

"Did you guys have fun at the party?"

What a question. I pondered it for a while before replying. "Yeah. Sort of."

"Cool. Catch you later," he said.

The day before semester break, there was another bombshell.

We were all sitting around in homeroom, when the dean walked in and asked to talk to Whitney. Whitney gave Georgia and Trish a look, like, *Who me?* And it's probably nothing. Whitney's parents make huge donations to Gros. But everyone was whispering excitedly. Whitney didn't come back to classes the whole day either.

I saw Isobel at the end of the day by the lockers. She had changed into another crazy outfit, this one involving bright Hawaiian prints on a tank top underneath her regulation button-down. She had a huge grin on her face.

"What's up?"

"Don't you know?"

"No!"

"*Incroya—*"

"Isobel! Tell me! Oh God, is it something about the web site again?"

"Whitney got suspended!" Isobel cheered.

Apparently, several of the other girls on the "slut" list had very angry parents who made a lot of noise and registered complaints about the notorious web site. The advanced computer class did a little Internet digging, and they figured out who had put it up before lunch.

"She paid for the site with her dad's credit card! What an imbecile!" Isobel shook her head. "She should have known she would get caught."

"So what happened?"

"The dean got really mad. They threatened to kick her out, because, you know, the whole Grosvernor Code of Conduct. But in the end they just gave her a warning and suspended her for a month."

"Suspended? Who cares? That's like a vacation."

"Yeah and it's Christmas break soon anyway, so she won't even miss anything."

"Big deal."

Isobel arched her eyebrow. "Well, it does mean she's not allowed to participate in school activities . . ."

"You mean?"

Isobel nodded.

The Soirée. The Montclair Academy–Grosvernor School winter ball that Whitney had so meticulously planned, with the whole *Titanic* theme. Speaking of sunken ships.

For the first time that day, I laughed.

"V, I have to tell you something," Isobel said, with a suddenly serious look on her face.

"You do?"

"Yeah."

"Don't be mad."

"Why? What is it?"

"It's, uh, about Claude," she said, a guilty flush on her cheeks.

And suddenly, I knew what she was going to tell me. I had known all along.

"He asked me to go to the Soirée with him," Isobel said, blushing more.

"That's great!" I said, feeling a little sad nonetheless. Even if I didn't like him anymore, it was still difficult to hear he liked someone else, even if that someone else was my best friend.

"Really? But I thought you had a mad crush on him?"

"Nah."

"Are you sure?"

"Uh-huh. Claude's not really my type anyway."

She gave me a quick, close hug—a real one this time, without the fancy air kisses.

"So maybe we can double-date, then! With you and Freddie, since you're going."

"I can't," I said. "I told you, I'm grounded."

"Oh no!" She frowned. "It won't be the same without you."

"It's all right. I don't feel like going anyway."

"Want a ride?" she asked, motioning to her Vespa.

"To the BART station? Sure," I said.

I held on to the back of Isobel's purple jacket all the way to Market Street. We coasted along up and down the steep hills of San Francisco. Sailboats were docked in the bay, and the Golden Gate Bridge glowed in the sunset. It was a beautiful day in December. The air was crisp and there was a smell of chestnuts in the air. I only had a light jacket over my blazer, but I wasn't at all cold.

GOOGLE CACHED LIST:

www.topfiveslutsatgrosvernorschool.com

1. Vicenza Arambullo

2. Stacey Bennett

3. Monica Wong

4. Claudia Jenkins

5. Elyse Russell

THIS SITE HAS BEEN TAKEN DOWN UNTIL FURTHER
NOTICE.

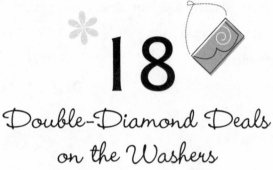

18

Double-Diamond Deals on the Washers

AFTER FINALS, SCHOOL let out for Christmas break, otherwise known as Ski Week, when all the rich families took their kids to Vail, Aspen, or Sun Valley. Of course, I was headed for the slopes of the Sears cafeteria. Which was fine, since it's not like anyone in my family knows how to ski anyway. But I hoped it wouldn't turn out to be so bad. After Claude asked Isobel to the Soirée, Isobel convinced her family not to spend three weeks in France like they always did, so she could stay in the city and attend the Soirée. I'd promised to help her find a ball dress if Mom ever let me out of the house again.

Mom still wasn't speaking to me, which was hard. We had never been mad at each other this long. Plus, Paul continued to avoid the cafeteria. If he didn't want to see me, then I didn't want to see him either. Still, I did miss him. I hadn't noticed how boring it was at the cafeteria without him. Before, I had always looked forward to his visits. Now the day stretched out for hours without any flavor or friendship.

The good news was that after my grandmother bribed the judge, who was an old friend of my late grandfather, all charges against Cousin Norbert and his video stores were dropped and our reality-tape smuggling business was back, stronger than ever. Dad's checks were accepted at Costco, and he was even able to take out a loan for a little seed money to launch a new cafeteria. He had finally succeeded in persuading the JCPenney store manager to let us open an employees' cafeteria in their store across the mall.

The bad news was that one of my new tasks was to push a loaded cart of supplies from Sears to JCPenney, from one end of the mall to the other. The cart always clacked loudly on the fake cobblestone floor, and there was nothing I hated more than the stares from all the puzzled strangers as I pushed an oversized grocery cart out in public. I despaired of ever being cool.

One afternoon Dad helped me load the cart, promising to hold down the fort while I made my delivery.

"Tell Mom I'm going to stop by there when you come back," Dad said.

I nodded and steeled myself for the ritual of mortification as I left the cocoonlike safety of the Sears back office and emerged in the blazingly cheerful, fluorescent-lit center of the mall. I wheeled by Ann Taylor, Express, Jeans West, and Contempo, wishing for the nth time that I was just an anonymous salesclerk folding sweaters instead of some glorified delivery girl. I noticed a skinny guy in an Incubus T-shirt sitting on one of the brick benches. I swerved to avoid a pile of trash on the floor, and a few items from the cart fell out. I swore softly as I tried to maintain my composure.

"Here."

I looked up and saw that it was Paul picking up a few stray oranges. He ran after a melon that rolled off to the side.

"Thanks," I said, putting the fruit back. "By the way—I wanted to ask you . . ." I said. But when I looked up, he was gone.

Well. So much for that. I craned my neck to try to see where he had disappeared to, but he wasn't anywhere. I sighed and continued my snail's pace, careful not to lose control of the cart this time.

The JCPenney store was a lot like Sears, except the cafeteria was located on the second floor instead of the ground level. The cafeteria was a tiny little corner in a back room. Unlike in the Sears store, we didn't have our own private back room where Mom could cook hot food and where I liked to hide from our customers. My parents had set up a little table with a cash register, rented a professional glass-door fridge, bought a microwave, and hung up a blackboard. I smiled when I saw the Daily

Specials sign and Dad's customary "Havanada!" greeting. It was five o'clock, and there was not a soul in the cafeteria.

"Hi, Mom," I said awkwardly. We had hardly exchanged a word to each other since the big fight. She had reluctantly given me back my computer when I told her I needed to use it for homework for finals, but my cell phone was still in lockdown, as was my modem connection. "Dad says he's going to come visit when I return to Sears."

"Okay," she said.

I helped her put the bags and boxes away in the tiny storage closet behind the fridge. As she turned to hand me the soup warmers, I noticed she was crying.

"What's wrong?" I asked.

"Nothing," she said, shaking her head.

"C'mon, Mom. Don't cry, please."

"I can't believe you haven't apologized to me."

"I apologized to you that night!"

She shook her head. "But you didn't come up to my room to see me afterward. I was waiting for you, and you never came."

I had always seen my mother as this larger-than-life presence. She was the most glamorous person I knew—and her wit and her tongue were sharp, I myself had not been immune to her lashings. I never really saw her as a person. I only knew her as my mother. But when I looked at her, so tiny in her dark blue apron, I realized then that she was having as much, if not more trouble, adjusting to life in America than I was. I was fourteen. She was forty. We both had a long way to go.

"I love you, Mom. You know I do," I said, starting to cry myself and letting all the pent-up feeling of the last weeks out in a rush. It was just too hard—the silence; the awkwardness; the long, quiet nights when I locked myself in my room while she watched television alone downstairs because Daddy was still at work and Brittany was already asleep.

"*Sige na, sige na,*" Mom said. (It's okay. It's okay.)

We held each other tightly. I didn't want to let go. I didn't know if I was forgiven, but I was glad to be hugged.

Afterward, Mom said, "You know, we can't return that dress, but we could try to get another one."

"It's all right, Mom. I don't want to go to the Soirée anyway." This time, I wasn't lying.

FROM: queen_vee@aol.com

TO: amparo.dellarosa@info.ph.com

SENT: Monday, December 14, 6:45 PM

SUBJECT: hellooo, stranger!

Dear Peaches,

What's up? Sorry I've been MIA. Total drama this week. Claude and I broke up. And I'm fine. It's no big deal. I realized he really wasn't the guy for me anyway. The semester's done, but I'm just going to stay home and help Mom at our restaurant. Nothing much to report. Dad says we might be able to come home next year for Christmas! But who knows? Dad always promises things that don't always come true. But that's okay. I think sometimes he just says nice things to make us all feel better. Anyway, that sucks your parents decided to go to Europe for break instead of coming to visit here.

Love,

V

19
One Woman's Trash Is Another's Treasure

CHRISTMAS AT SEARS meant all the salesclerks wore white sweatshirts emblazoned with red stockings that declared NAUGHTY! or NICE! or FILL 'ER UP! Some of the clerks even donned red fluffy Santa hats with puffy pom-poms on the ends.

At first I was repulsed, thinking about how at Grosvernor we had celebrated the holidays by singing French noëls in the Belvedere. But by the next weekend I had gotten into the spirit of things and I went to work wearing white stockings that read MERRY CHRISTMAS on the right leg and HAPPY NEW YEAR on the left one. If you can't beat 'em, join 'em.

But I wasn't at Sears a lot. Once school let out, almost every day I took the train into the city so I could accompany Isobel to almost every designer boutique in town. Mom and Dad hired their first employee, a Filipino immigrant who was a cousin of a friend of a coworker of Freddie's mom, who had just moved to San Francisco. I was finally free.

Isobel and I went to Macy's, Neiman Marcus, and Saks and looked at everything, from voluminous princessy dresses to sleek pantsuits. At the Gucci store on Union Square, Isobel convinced me to try on dresses as well, even though I had nowhere to wear them. The salesclerks glared at us the whole time, but Isobel was blithely oblivious to the fact, and kept picking out thousand-dollar dresses from the racks. It was the same at Yves Saint Laurent and Chanel. Isobel knew her parents would never buy her such an expensive dress, but she said it was criminal the way they didn't let you even try them on even if you weren't buying them. "Fashion should be for everybody," she said.

At Vera Wang, I sat on plush velvet-covered cushions waiting for Isobel as she tried on her dresses for the Soirée. She disappeared into a dressing room with a few choice pieces.

"What do you think?"

I looked up expecting to find Isobel and instead saw Carter O'Riordan, who was trying on a heavenly peach-colored column gown. "Is it too much?" she asked underneath folds of chiffon.

"It's so pretty," I said, flattered she would ask my opinion.

Isobel walked out in a strapless number and said hi to Carter.

"Are you guys going to the dance?" Carter asked.

"I'm not," I said, shaking my head.

"*Oui*, I am." Isobel nodded.

"Right. With Claude." She smiled and turned to me. "Too bad you aren't coming. Margy McCarthy's having a big after-ball party at her beach house in Marin. You should come," Carter said, examining her silhouette in the mirror.

"Maybe we will," Isobel said.

"What about you, Vicenza?"

"Me? Nah. It's okay."

"I mean, even if you don't feel like going to the ball, I totally get it. But you can always just come to the party. I wouldn't even go to this thing, but my mom is totally making me," she said, rolling her eyes.

"I'll think about it," I allowed, smiling.

Isobel shook her head at the black strapless dress and emerged a few minutes later from the dressing room wearing a wedding dress complete with a big, poofy, cupcakelike skirt and a lengthy train.

"What is that?" I asked.

"It was left in the dressing room. I couldn't resist!" Isobel giggled.

"Now that is a dress," Carter agreed. "But if you wear that, I think Claude is going to have a heart attack."

* * *

The next afternoon, disgusted with the slim pickings at all the shops, we hit every thrift store in the city, but when nothing turned up, I took her to the Salvation Army in South San Francisco.

"This is the best!" Isobel said, filling her basket with groovy 70s style tracksuits, dirndl skirts, wool gauchos, and a vintage Hermès bag. "How come you never inform me about this place?"

We each left with tie-neck polka-dot blouses, embroidered cardigan sweaters with mink collars, and a pair of 40s-style Mary Jane shoes.

But no Soirée dress.

Nothing. We came up empty. We just couldn't find the Dress. They were all too short or too long, too big or too tight. Or not Gallic enough. It seemed a completely hopeless enterprise. Until the day before the Soirée, when I suddenly got a *brilliant* idea. . . .

This time Isobel took the train all the way out to the suburbs to visit me at Sears, and I had fun showing her all the cool things about my job. She couldn't believe there was so much food at our cafeteria—and that she could eat anything she wanted. She stuffed herself full of pastrami sandwiches, and I even taught her how to work the register. She gave everybody a cheerful *"Bonjour"* when they walked in. After we closed up shop, we took the bus to my house.

"Your house is so cute," she said. "I love all the patio furniture in the living room. *C'est très avant-garde!*"

I grinned, happy that Isobel didn't think we were freaks. I didn't mention that plastic furniture was all that we could afford.

"Come on up," I said, and took her to my room. "I have something for you."

I pulled it out of the closet and showed her.

"Do you think you can maybe do something with this?" I asked.

An hour later, Isobel put on the DRESS.

"You look gorgeous," I told her.

"You think?" she asked, pursing her lips.

"It's *insane*."

She was wearing the same dress Mom had bought me to wear to the Soirée but with a few Isobel-style variations. She had made dozens of vertical slashes in the hem, so instead of three proper layers, there was just one crazy explosion of tulle. And she had moved the butt bow, sewing it in a crossover style on the front bustline. It was crazy, kooky, wild, and very French. It looked perfect on her.

"Are you sure you don't mind?" she asked.

"No, it's a gift. Take it."

"I can't believe that all this time you owned this amazing dress!"

"Well, actually, my mom picked it out."

The last day of break, Isobel and I went to see Claude play lacrosse in the final championship. Since he passed geometry for the first semester, he was off academic probation and back on the team. I'd gotten my own grades in the mail, and was happy to see I passed geometry I with a B. Dad joked that it ruined the perfect pattern of my straight A's, but I was relieved to have kept my scholarship. We saw Tess, Freddie's girlfriend, in the stands and went up to sit next to her. I guessed she was there to see Freddie, who was still managing the team.

"GO WILDCATS!!!" Isobel cheered, waving her orange-and-blue pom-poms wildly.

Claude looked up and waved when he saw us in the bleachers.

It was kind of weird not to be in love with him anymore. It left me feeling a little empty, since there was no one to fantasize about. No more writing my name with his in my notebooks or wondering if our kids would inherit his nose and my hair color. But it was gratifying to see how happy he and Isobel were. She said she would even teach him how to hold his liquor. She was French, so she knew all about that.

A thunderous cheer exploded from the opposing side. The St. Stephen team was running up the field, passing the ball between them expertly, and the forward shot the ball straight for the Montclair net. It flew in an arc, and seemed a sure hit. The crowd gasped, then erupted in cheers when the Wildcats goalie caught it just in time.

"Good save!" Isobel bellowed. "GOOOO, FRED!!!!"

"Fred?" I asked.

"Yeah, your friend Fred? He's on the team."

"As like, the towel boy, duh."

"What are you talking about?" She shot me an incredulous look. "He's the goalie."

I looked up at the field doubtfully. Freddie? The goalie who just executed that magnificent save? At halftime, the goalie took off his mask, and it was definitely Freddie underneath. He really was on the team. He was a Montclair jock all along, and actually deserved to wear that varsity jacket.

Freddie waved at us and Claude clapped him on the shoulder, handing him a Styrofoam cup of water.

"Claude said he'd been having problems with his knee so he's been on the bench all season, managing the team," Isobel told me.

Later, Freddie told me that the reason he was so secretive about his girlfriend was because his parents hadn't wanted him to date before college, and he didn't want me blabbing to my parents about his love life. But they had finally come around to accepting Tess, the beauty queen. Apparently no one was ever good enough for their son, but after he threatened to throw away the Harvard acceptance, they had caved. Freddie and Tess and Claude and Isobel were double-dating to the Soirée.

"You know, Tuna still doesn't have a date," Isobel said, meaning the hulky defensive guard on the team who had carried a case of beer to Claude's party.

"I don't want to go with Tuna," I said.

I knew exactly who I wished I could ask to the Soirée. But it was too late. He didn't want anything to do with me.

FROM: queen_vee@aol.com

TO: amparo.dellarosa@info.ph.com

SENT: Thursday, December 17, 4:32 PM

SUBJECT: bonjour!

Hi Peaches,

So this week Isobel and I—wait, I've told you about her haven't I? She's this really funny French girl that I'm really good friends with. You'd like her, P., she dresses like you. Anyway, we went to all these boutiques and department stores and thrift stores to look for a dress for Isobel to wear to the Soirée, but she just borrowed one of mine. Remember how we used to always wear each other's clothes? Anyway, I'm not going because Claude and I broke up and I really can't be bothered to find another date. I'll probably just stay home and watch *Saturday Night Live*.

Love,

V

20
Elle's All That

ISOBEL WANTED ME to help her get ready for the dance, so on the night of Soirée, Dad dropped me off at her house. I helped her with her hair and curled her eyelashes the way she had taught me.

"Ouch!" she said.

"You must suffer to be beautiful!" I joked.

Isobel's mom knocked on the door. "How's everything in there, chérie? Claude *est ici*."

I peeked out the door and saw Claude standing in Isobel's living room, grinning at the Eminem poster and holding a corsage. Isobel walked down the stairs as if in slow motion. When he looked up to see her, his eyes shone with admiration. I made a point of playing "Kiss Me" on Isobel's iMac speakers as she made her entrance. I gave her the momentous *She's All That* moment I had been wanting forever. And she hadn't even needed a makeover—she looked exactly like she always did.

Claude pinned a bouquet on her dress and kissed her gently on the cheek. She blushed and handed him his boutonniere.

I followed her down the stairs.

"You look great," I told her wistfully.

"V, you're not going?" Claude asked.

"No, I don't have a date," I said honestly.

"Don't worry, it's not a big deal—it's just a stupid dance." He shrugged.

"I know," I said.

Isobel's parents took so many digital photos they almost blinded the happy couple.

"Are you sure you don't want to meet us at the after party?" Isobel asked wistfully.

"No, really, I'll be okay. Go. Have fun!"

They left in a cloud of her perfume.

I said good night to the Saint-Pierre's and walked over to the curb where Dad was waiting for me.

"Hey," I said. "I wasn't too long, was I?"

I opened the door and realized that my whole family was in the van to pick me up. They were all staring at me when I climbed inside. I wondered what they were all doing there. We were just turning around and driving back to the suburbs anyway.

"What?"

They were silent. Then Dad said happily, "C'mon, we're going out to the movies! My treat!"

The line at the movie theater was filled with tons of kids my age, sticking their tongues down their boyfriends' throats or running around in large, boisterous groups, but I didn't notice. I waited contentedly in the ticket line with my family. They would probably embarrass me again sometime in the near future, like, say, tomorrow, but for now, I was satisfied with their company.

When the line crept forward, I noticed the boy in front of us was wearing a ratty brown work shirt. I could recognize those shoulders anywhere. He walked up to the counter. "One for the Stephen King please."

"Paul," I said, touching his arm.

He turned. "Hey."

"Hey."

"What are you doing here?"

"As usual, hanging out with my family," I said. "What else do I do?"

Mom looked up at the list. "Do you want to go see the fish movie? It's the only thing Brittany can see," she asked.

I shook my head.

"Oh, hi, Paul," she said. "I haven't seen you in the cafeteria much—we miss you."

"Thanks, Mrs. A. I cut back on my hours to study for the SATs. What are you guys up to tonight?"

"Well, we're going to go see the fish movie. But I don't know what V is doing."

"You didn't get me a ticket?" I asked.

"No, I thought maybe you want to see something with Paul?"

I was in shock. Mom was actually encouraging me to hang out *alone* with a boy?

"Up to you." Paul shrugged.

"Sure. I mean, if you and Dad don't mind," I said.

"Mind? Why would we mind?" She elbowed Dad. Dad shrugged. "We know Paul. Do you drive?" she asked, turning to Paul.

Paul nodded. "I brought the Batmobile."

"You know the way home. He can take you home after the movies. By eleven."

I couldn't believe it. Mom arranging my first date! And I wasn't turning fifteen until next week! This was so disconcerting, except it wasn't.

Paul went up to the ticket counter. "Can I get another please?"

I kissed Mom and Dad on the cheek, patted Brit on the head, and ran after him into the theater.

Mom had passed me a twenty-dollar bill, so we shared the most gigantic tub of the LARGEST size popcorn swimming in hot butter (or really, butter flavoring). And two medium Cokes. His hand brushed mine every time he grabbed a handful. I think it was on purpose.

"Hey, I almost forgot," he said, between sips of Coke. "I got this for you. Have you read it yet?"

He pulled a hardcover copy of the latest Dark Tower novel out of his backpack. I'd told him I wanted to read it a while back. "Just let me finish reading it and it's yours," he'd told me.

"You're not mad at me anymore?" I asked.

"Well, I was a little upset you forgot about our date. But I figured, who am I to tell you what to do."

"It was a crazy month. I'm really sorry."

"Seriously, it's not a big deal."

"It is to me." I looked him right in the eye. He has the nicest green eyes, a warm, yellow green that turned blue in certain light. He kind of looked like Tobey Mag—oh, forget about Tobey. He was cuter than Tobey. He was here, he was sitting next to me. He was a real boy, not one from posters on my bedroom walls.

Then he did the craziest thing. He just leaned over and kissed me. Just like that. His lips were soft and buttery. I closed my eyes and I couldn't even breathe.

"Okay," he said, as the house lights dimmed and the trailers rolled.

FROM: queen_vee@aol.com

TO: amparo.dellarosa@info.ph.com

SENT: Sunday, December 20, 12:32 AM

SUBJECT: that in-the-rain-kiss

Dear Peaches,

   You know when Mary Jane discovers it's really Peter Parker she's in love with? That's how I feel. Seriously. I know I say this all the time, but this time it's TRUE. Friday night I went to the movies with this boy, and it was the best night of my life. I'll tell you all about it later, because I really need to go to sleep now. But I hope you get to meet him sometime.

Miss you.

Love,

V

WWW.WELOVECLAUDECALIGARI.COM

Sighted! C.C. at the Winter Soirée with his new girlfriend—
a French import! Just the ticket since our guy and his date
were voted *roi et reine* of the ball! Congratulations, Claude!
Remember the little people! Check out new pics from the
after party in Marin! Members, don't forget, dues are due
next month! Until the next C.C. sighting! Ciao!

Hi, Peaches!

So, my dad finally won the lottery yesterday! $50!
We celebrated by having dinner at P. F. Chang. It's a chain
restaurant with Asian food and it's really good! Paul is
the new guy I'm seeing. He's a stock boy at Sears, where
we have our restaurant—but it's not really a restaurant—
it's more like a cafeteria. Actually, it's the employees'
cafeteria at Sears. BTW, did you notice *Teen Vogue* did
a top-10 story of the latest looks—and nude stockings
are now the "it" hue of the season.

I know my e-mails are always so short, but I promise,
in the future, I'll write you long and detailed letters.

Love,

V